PEN

TIME AND TIME AGAIN

B. M. Gill is the author of *Nursery Crimes*, *The Twelfth Juror*, *Seminar for Murder*, *Suspect*, and *Death Drop*. Her novel *Dying to Meet You* will be published later this year. Winner of Britain's top crime-writing award, the prestigious Gold Dagger, she is a three-time Edgar nominee. She lives in North Wales.

TIME AND TIME AGAIN

B. M. Gill

PENGUIN BOOKS

PENGUIN BOOKS
Published by the Penguin Group
Viking Penguin, a division of Penguin Books USA Inc.,
375 Hudson Street, New York, New York 10014, U.S.A.
Penguin Books Ltd, 27 Wrights Lane,
London W8 5TZ, England
Penguin Books Australia Ltd, Ringwood,
Victoria, Australia
Penguin Books Canada Ltd, 2801 John Street,
Markham, Ontario, Canada L3R 1B4
Penguin Books (N.Z.) Ltd, 182–190 Wairau Road,
Auckland 10, New Zealand

Penguin Books Ltd, Registered Offices:
Harmondsworth, Middlesex, England

First published in Great Britain by Hodder & Stoughton Limited 1989
First published in the United States of America
by Charles Scribner's Sons, an imprint
of Macmillan Publishing Company, 1990
Published in Penguin Books 1991

1 3 5 7 9 10 8 6 4 2

This is a work of fiction. Names, characters, places, and incidents either
are the product of the author's imagination or are used fictitiously. Any
resemblance to actual events or persons, living or dead, is entirely coincidental.

LIBRARY OF CONGRESS CATALOGING IN PUBLICATION DATA
Gill, B. M.
Time and time again/B. M. Gill.
p. cm. — (Penguin crime fiction)
ISBN 0 14 01.4360 2
I. Title.
PR6057.I538T5 1991
823'.914—dc20 90–43840

Printed in the United States of America

TIME AND TIME AGAIN

1

Freedom tastes of sharp morning air. The seven o'clock sun is casting a pale, frosty haze over the farmlands. It's very cold. I'm shivering in my Italian tailored suit, not worn since the trial, and it's too tight. Eighteen months of stodge. And my shoes are killing me. Why are open prisons built on gritty country roads? Why do they let us out so early in the morning? Why don't I feel elated, euphoric, even just plain happy? Why, for God's sake, am I so jumpy, so alarmed?

Alarmed is the wrong word. Uneasy . . .? That's not right either. But closer.

Rene, standing beside me, muffled up in a cosy scarlet anorak, is reacting normally. Calm. Smiling.

A motorbike humming somewhere in the distance bursts into a triumphant roar as it turns the corner. "Here's Olly," she says.

He's Olly when she speaks of him affectionately. "That bloody creep, Oliver," when he failed to write. Her face now, as she watches him getting off his red Kawasaki motorbike, is aglow. He's her husband, she told me after one of his visits, not common-law, full church rites.

As Christopher is mine.

I never call him Chris.

Will he be here soon? Has something happened to the car? To him? What do I do if he doesn't come? Go back inside and telephone for a taxi? Tell the screw my husband has ditched me? No way. Panic is making me rigid. I can't move.

Rene, my unlikely friend, becomes aware of my distress. "Olly and I will stay around," she says, "until he shows."

He does show. Almost immediately.

We still have the same Audi, I notice. On his last visit he talked of changing it. It's funny the things you talk about on visiting days. Things that don't matter much. And your eyes don't meet.

Our eyes aren't meeting now. He's walking over to me, embracing me, and I'm looking over his shoulder at Oliver and Rene. They're holding hands. Christopher is kissing my forehead, rather perfunctorily, not my lips. The kind of gesture a priest might make to a penitent. Bless you, my child, all is forgiven.

In our case a stockbroker greeting his recalcitrant wife.

"Welcome," he says, and then "Happy birthday . . . Glad the Press aren't here."

My birthday? I'd forgotten. It's the thirteenth of February and I'm twenty-seven today. My twenty-sixth birthday was spent inside. I refuse to remember it. The Press? Surely they exhausted the topic ages ago?

We're walking towards the car and Rene and Oliver are getting on to his powerful-looking machine. Our possessions, signed for and collected, all the red tape of release duly observed, are in a couple of large carrier bags. She's managed to stuff the contents of hers into a haversack. Awkward on a motorbike, but they seem to be managing. He has given her a white helmet which hides her bright red curls. She fastens it then calls out to me, "See you, Maeve. Thanks for everything." I say the same. "See you. Thanks for everything, too."

Neither of us knows exactly what we mean by this. A friendship untouched by sex, and with very little mental affinity, has somehow been warming. We like each other. It's that simple.

Oliver turns briefly and looks at me. They're a striking contrast. Rene, flamboyant. He, thin, sombre-eyed, like Ford Madox Brown's emigrant. I focus my memory on Brown's *The Last of*

8

England painting, escaping into my head as I do when I'm embarrassed, or frightened, or too confused by events to be rational.

Christopher goes ahead of me to the car and puts my carrier bag in the boot. Then, meticulously polite as ever, he opens the passenger door for me. "One of your lot?" he asks as we both watch the bike gathering speed and belching exhaust fumes.

Rene, her body pressed curvaciously into Oliver's back, waves awkwardly. I wave, too. "My lot?" I know what he means, but pretend I don't.

"Your CND buddies."

Buddies sounds derogatory, as it's meant to. I tell him that Rene has all the virtues that I lack. A girl of sound common sense, happy to see the world go bang.

"What was Rene in for, then?" He breaks the name up into two syllables, correctly, but not the way she pronounces it.

"Rene, as in 'mean'," I tell him. "Only she isn't."

He gets into the driving seat, frowning, obviously bothered that I might have associated with 'undesirables'. "Self-sufficiency and strength of mind should see you through," he told me when I was sentenced. "Keep yourself to yourself, Maeve. With remission you'll serve about eighteen months. It will pass quickly."

He should try it!

I tell him that Rene made fraudulent claims from the DHSS. "If she'd had my training she could have nicked a lot more."

I'm deliberately needling him. I can't help it. I'm sorry. I keep remembering all the old jibes. Even the judge had a go at me. "That a professional woman – a chartered accountant – with an impeccable background – should behave with such lunacy – such mindless hooliganism and brutality – is almost beyond belief."

It had taken Rene to put it into perspective.

"You got caught up in the mob," she said. "Missiles got thrown. You didn't mean to clobber anybody, but with that sort of build-up of the fuzz it would be remarkable if one of them hadn't got in the way. Lots of others got hurt, too. It just so happened that they picked on you. You're not brutal. You're just daft."

And that was the start of the friendship. Words I needed to

hear – brusque, but kindly. They helped. Not a lot. I still had nightmares. I still do. Probably always will.

"I hope she doesn't mean it," Christopher says as he starts the engine.

"What?"

"About seeing you."

I don't answer. We have exchanged addresses, but there's no need to tell Christopher that. I wonder what sort of conversation she is having now with Oliver, if it's possible to converse on a motorbike. Between gasps for air, is he telling her he loves her very much? They seemed pleased to be together.

After we have been driving for some while in almost total silence Christopher suggests we have breakfast at The Wheatsheaf – just an hour away from our London home. "Did you have anything to eat before they let you out?"

I tell him I had a cup of tea. I don't tell him I'm not hungry. Obviously he is or he wouldn't have thought of it. The last meal we had at The Wheatsheaf was on our first wedding anniversary four years ago. He probably won't remember.

But he does.

"We sat at the same table then," he says, as the waitress shows us over to the green and gold papered alcove near the fireplace. In the morning light it looks pretentious, slightly tatty.

"When?" I pretend not to remember.

He knows I'm pretending.

"Maeve – it's all right. Just a bad time that's over." He reaches across and touches my hand. I force myself not to withdraw. I want to cry and turn my head away.

I'm served with grapefruit which I manage to eat. And a small piece of toast with marmalade. Christopher has the lot: eggs, bacon, sausage. At times of stress he used to smoke too much. Now that he's given up tobacco he over-eats. He has put on weight, but it suits him. He's an attractive man. I'm looking at him now as if he doesn't belong to me. Well, he doesn't, of course. Nobody belongs to anybody. I mean I'm looking at him dispassionately. He has good features. A little grey in the brown hair. Eyes that are too keen if they latch on to you. So far, I haven't let them.

He raises them. I look away. "Your mother baked a cake," he says.

This is a puzzling comment. My mother has baked many cakes. She's good at it. Likes doing it. My mother, unlike me, is domesticated.

"And so?" I shrug.

"For your birthday," he explains. "She drove over with it yesterday."

"And is still at home?" I ask, alarmed.

I love my mother, but not today.

"No. She left it. She understands we need to be alone for a while."

I think about this. Alone to go to bed together – after a long period of abstinence – well, on my part, and most probably on Christopher's. I wonder how it will be. I feel a million years removed from him.

"When you do see her she won't harass you." He tries to sound reassuring. "The cake is a kind of peace offering. No more talk about disgrace and your father spinning in his grave and all that rubbish." He smiles at me and this time our eyes do meet and we're able to communicate and not just mouth sentences at each other. "She calls what happened an aberration," he goes on. "As good a word as any, I suppose. Apparently one of your father's Irish forebears did something similar – way back in time. The gene, therefore, is on your father's side. The Irish are an unpredictable lot."

I feel weepy now about my father. He was gentle and kindly. Only he would understand my sense of guilt.

I ask how Sergeant Sutherland is.

Christopher pours coffee for the two of us before answering. I wait. Frightened.

At last he tells me. "His vision is impaired. The stone, or whatever it was you threw, caught him full in the face. Well, you knew that. But you didn't blind him. If you had he'd have been pensioned out of the Force. He's been transferred to the Met. A desk job." He pauses, then goes on briskly. "You've got to get it into your head that it wasn't a deliberate assault, it was a reflex action when things started getting rough. If you hadn't been involved in those stupid earlier confrontations at Greenham Common you wouldn't have been dealt with so severely. The judge made an example of you."

I point out, as I have so many times before, that there was no connection between Langdon village and Greenham Common. He disagrees, "It was civil disobedience in both cases."

The penalty for my civil disobedience at Greenham Common had been imprisonment or a fine. Christopher, despite my warning him not to, had paid the fine. More aggro when we got home. He had apologised for deflating the balloon of my egotism with the pin-prick of common sense. He can use awfully silly phrases when he's cross.

"I was born in Langdon," I remind him bitterly. "I lived there until I was ten. I had a right to go there. To protest. Why should they use a beautiful place like that to bury their nuclear waste? They were poisoning the land, now and for evermore. They had to be stopped."

"But not violently."

"We didn't expect violence. We just formed a human chain against the excavators getting through. It wasn't my crowd who stirred up trouble with the police. And it wasn't the villagers. I don't know how the violence erupted. A lot of brainless yobs got in on the act – a change from soccer violence, perhaps. Come kick a few anti-nuke freaks, and draw blood from the fuzz while you're at it. Stir it, boys, stir it. All good clean fun. Christ, it was like a storm suddenly breaking." My hand holding the coffee cup is trembling and I can't put the cup back on to the saucer without knocking the rim.

Christopher takes it from me and replaces it neatly. "You get too emotional. Too involved. Learn to stand back and let things happen to other people. You can't stop the unstoppable. A social conscience can be a curse when it's allied to your kind of temperament. You over-react. Hurt yourself. Others."

"Have you seen him? Seen Sergeant Sutherland?"

"No. He wouldn't wish to see me. Or you. The letter you wrote him was returned to me – torn up."

I am unsurprised. It was a feeble letter. An inarticulate mumbling of regret. Had I been him I would have returned it steeped in corrosive acid.

"Did he say anything – separately – to you?"

"No."

"You didn't tell me this before, on any of your visits."

"I didn't want to upset you. Not in a place like that."

"Then you know how I feel?"

"Don't be silly, Maeve. Of course I know."

For a moment or two we look at each other mutely.

We arrived at our South London home at just after eleven. The house, mellow with sunlight on weathered brick, looked inviting until I saw the blue Ford Granada parked at the top of the drive and partially hidden by the shrubbery. The Press hadn't lost interest after all. A large young man, seated next to the driver, got out and ambled over to us, smiling falsely. He presented his Press card. His editor had sent him along, he said, as if apologising for trespass committed by someone else, just to ask a few questions and get my reaction to being 'outside' again. He wouldn't keep me long.

Christopher, less put out than I, apparently expecting something like this to happen, told him suavely that I had nothing to say, that I was rather tired, and asked him to leave.

The reporter, who must have played this scene many times before, stood his ground. "What does it feel like being free, Mrs. Barclay?"

It was the usual silly question. What does it feel like, sir, madam, when your house is burnt to the ground – when you're dug out from under a landslide – when your nearest and dearest are dead? Or – on a more mundane level – when you're let out of gaol?

I wondered what the stock answer was, but obeyed Christopher's unspoken command to remain silent and went indoors. Let Christopher handle it. There are times when I value his protection and snuggle into it like an old coat.

He joined me in the hall in just a few minutes and put his arm across my shoulder. "It doesn't do to antagonise the Press, but there are limits. Let's hope you won't be bothered again. Welcome home."

Home.

I've thought about it, dreamed about it, longed for it and now I am here it feels different, smaller than I remember but far more plush. Soft-toned Aubusson carpets, heavy velvet curtains in shades of bronze and apricot, Waterford crystal and antique china, impossibly frail. I don't think I like the pictures on the walls any more – sophisticated juxtaposition of squares and blobs, make of them what you will, anything or nothing. At this moment – nothing.

I take a walk out into the back garden, a private place where Press cars aren't able to intrude. Christopher has planted a mass of red crocus tulips near the white winter heather, or got Walker the part-time gardener to do it. And the shed has been tidied. The cobwebbed corners I couldn't bear to go near have been swept clean. My husband, so my mother tells me, is a jewel amongst men. And most of my friends agree. The comparison they're making between us is obvious. I wonder if any of the more nubile ones have offered him consolation.

As yet no one has mentioned divorce.

I stand in the middle of the green, dewy lawn and think about freedom. An impossible concept.

When I go back indoors I prowl around the house for a while, running my fingers along the books on the shelves, touching the bottles of scent, talc and bath oil in the bathroom, noticing the loo paper is soft and pastel coloured. I resist the temptation of a long, hot bath and have a quick shower instead, then look in the wardrobe for something different to wear. The suit was a mistake. We wore mufti inside, anything we liked that was comfortable and easy, mostly shirts and jeans. One of the cons, Anna Horden, wore neat, dark dresses with embroidered collars. Beautiful, silent Anna, with the dazed-looking eyes, who seemed Madonna pure but surely couldn't have been. I select a green tailored dress that reminds me of her, but it fits as badly as the suit. I've become sloppy. I look the way I looked when I left school. Not fat, but not svelte either. Prison should thin you down, make you look wan. How is it I should feel starved inside my head and yet look the way I do? And my skin needs improving. They didn't starve us of fresh air, but my skin looks as if it needs to suck in sunlight. Do we respond physically to psychological pressure? Oh God, quit the self-analysis. Put on something nice and loose. I find my fluffy blue bedroom slippers and velvet housecoat and wear them to go downstairs.

Christopher is sitting in the living room. He has poured two glasses of champagne and we clink the glasses together in a gesture of forced bonhomie, and drink in silence. There is a great awkwardness, almost shyness, between us. We have forgotten how to talk together with ease for any length of time. It was better in the old days when he told me how goddamned stupid I was being. About everything. And I did a lot of yelling back.

Ours is a marriage of opposites. Our views differ on most matters of importance. Of importance to me. I committed myself to full membership of the CND on my eighteenth birthday. When we met and married a few years later and I insisted on attending the meetings he smiled indulgently at my 'folly'. When he became a Freemason, I smiled indulgently back. Now the smiles are wearing thin. His embarrassment when I cut the wires at Greenham Common must have been acute. And when I was put inside after Langdon it must have been hell for him. How did he respond to the sympathy of his conventional, law-abiding friends? I wonder. With a shrug of the shoulders? A tired smile? I tell him, by way of a belated apology, that it must have been difficult for him when I was 'away'. Nice, clean euphemism, 'away'. He replies, rather wryly, that all marriages have good and bad times. "The past is over. Forget it."

Impossible.

We're both afraid of going any deeper than this and so I open my birthday presents and look at my cards. His present to me is an emerald ring. Pretty. I slip it on. It shows up the roughness of my hands and my nails need attention. He notices and I sense compassion. "You must have had a hard time in there." I tell him it could have been worse. "There were chores to be done, but quite a lot of the screws were kind. And there were art classes and a library." I don't mention the frightening times, the sudden hysterical rages, the animosity and petty jealousy. I wasn't exactly 'picked on', but the Press hadn't helped with its description of my background, stupidly exaggerated. The emotional reaction to imprisonment is hard to describe, and better not dwelt on. It's better that Christopher shouldn't know how it really was. My pain is my own, I won't burden him with it.

He draws my attention back to the rest of the unopened gifts. "Come on, Maeve. This is a celebration of today. Let's see what you've got." He's being kind and tactful.

My mother's birthday present is a white silk nightdress heavy with lace, and even heavier with innuendo. "Here you are, darling," I can hear her saying. "You've been a very silly girl, but you've paid for your silliness, so go and make love to that wonderful husband of yours and make yourselves a baby."

"Very virginal," I say to Christopher. "Very honeymoonish."

He smiles. "When have you ever worn a nightdress?"

All the time I was in prison, I think, but not one like this.

2

Going to gaol is a culture shock. Coming out is a culture shock in reverse. My greatest need during the last couple of weeks has been privacy. I lock the bathroom door while I wallow in the bath. I wanted to lock the bedroom door, too, and spread myself in the luxury of the double bed. Only I couldn't. Actions can be read as statements and statements can be misread. Christopher sees a women's prison as a lesbian breeding ground. It is, for some. Some of the women were obvious dykes, especially the dominant partners. I remember seeing Maggie, who was in for arson and very butch with fair cropped hair and muscular legs, putting her arms around Anna, and Anna freezing up with horrified rejection. Maggie had cringed at the rebuff, then backed off, sulking. Some of the women watching had laughed. Two people hurt didn't seem much of a joke to me. Rene and I had to put up with speculative looks from time to time; were we lovers or weren't we? She thought this funny and I learnt not to care. We both need our men.

And so, that first night home, we made love. And because my body had been starved of sex it responded. The orgasm wasn't faked. It wasn't possible to utter the right words of love, though, or even try to. Christopher's love-making was never very articulate either, so he probably didn't notice. He slept quickly afterwards and I got up and warmed some milk for myself in the kitchen. The night is nice when there's no one else around. You can hear the clock tick, the soft swish of the rain.

My birthday cake had been left untouched on one of the work-tops and I cut myself a slice. My mother had iced it carefully, thin white lines of blue on white. They look rather like bars and remind me of Holloway. Security at Chornley Open Prison was less obvious. Visitors saw neat lawns and flower beds surrounding a red-bricked Victorian mansion and were reassured. Inside it had been converted into an up-to-date institution for low category risk prisoners. The cage might appear gilded externally but internally it was highly functional. A bird flying free would have been a more apt decoration. Knowing my mother, I am quite aware that no such thought occurred to her. She lacks imagination, my mum. Lucky woman.

She came to visit me on my second day home and after kissing me and telling me I looked pale we both stood in silence for a few moments. It's difficult to bridge a gap in time when the water under the bridge has been murky. She was the first to recover her poise and chatted quite tactfully about a lot of trivia before returning to the main topic. We were having coffee together in the living room when she handed me the *Daily Mail*. "There's a picture of you in it, darling. It's not in the *Telegraph* or the *Guardian*, so you probably haven't seen it."

The reporter must have taken the photograph from inside his car when we were getting out of ours. I'm in profile and look calm and assured as if I'm returning from a holiday at a swish hotel. It's almost flattering. Christopher, standing behind me, looks hunched up and weary and quite a lot older than thirty-seven. He could be taken for my father.

'*CND woman set free*' is the caption under it, followed by a short paragraph:

CND activist, Maeve Barclay (27) was tight lipped yesterday after her release from Chornley Open Prison. Jailed for 18 months for wounding a police sergeant at an anti-nuclear demo at Langdon village two years ago the blonde, elegant business woman spent her first day of freedom incarcerated in her stockbroker husband's imposing Georgian residence refusing to talk to the Press. Sergeant Robert Sutherland (48) married, with two young children, suffered severe facial and eye injuries.

I sat down on the window seat, feeling sick. Children. Two young children. I hadn't been told about them before. Had I shattered their lives, too? The air was heavy with the scent my mother uses and the old panic feeling of being unable to breathe made me struggle to take a few shallow breaths.

She sat beside me and patted my cold hand. "You had to expect publicity when you went in – and now you're out this should be the end of it. It could have been worse. They've stopped calling you Barclay. Elegant business woman isn't derogatory and the snap's a nice one."

"I didn't know he had children . . ."

"It was mentioned in some of the newspapers at the time. Christopher and I kept most of them from you. Notice how they remind everyone he's a stockbroker, and they call this house an imposing Georgian residence?"

"Which it isn't." (How old are his children? How young is young?)

"Well, it certainly isn't small – and it *is* Georgian. You're not so naïve that you don't understand what they're getting at. When women of your background behave like hookers it makes news. When hookers throw bricks no one takes any notice. They're not supposed to know any better."

I try to put his children out of my mind and concentrate on what she is saying. Hookers, I tell her, is American for prostitutes and does she think all CND members are call girls from the Big Apple? Lady Mary Jewson, for instance, currently secretary of the local branch?

My mother knows as well as I do that Mary is a true-blue Tory, a conformist on every issue except this one, and with enough brain power, as a Master of Science, to argue the opposition, of any colour or creed, into the ground.

She changes the subject and suggests that Christopher and I

should have a pleasant little holiday abroad somewhere. I tell her I have to get used to being here before I can get used to being anywhere else – and what kind of pleasant little holiday does she suppose Sergeant Sutherland has had with his family since I half blinded him?

Mother ignores this and mentions the happy time we had in Portugal with my father the year before he died. "You were sixteen then. Doing well at school. He was very proud of you."

I still love the memory of him and the ice melts a little when I think of him. He was a lapsed Catholic and I'm nothing – not even agnostic – but we both understood Fatima as we watched the pilgrims scraping along painfully on their knees to the shrine. "We punish ourselves according to our need," he told me then. That's true. I needed prison. I don't resent it. It scratched the surface of my pain. Without it I could have done myself more injury.

All this is difficult to express. To anybody.

The publicity in the *Mail* resulted in a lot of letters – some from people who knew me. Most condemned. A few were kind. One was so vicious it made me throw up. It was at this stage that Christopher took complete charge of my mail and I was glad to let him. He destroyed it all – even, I suspect, the approving ones. He didn't approve of the approvers and so protected me from everyone. He couldn't do anything about what he called the 'floral tributes' though. Most of these were from the Langdon villagers and I put them in every available vase and ignored him when he said I'd turned the place into a funeral parlour.

There are flowers in hospitals, too. People sometimes get better. In time you stop wanting to die.

Two things happened yesterday. I drove the car – my own mini – out on to the road and was so nervous of the traffic that I returned almost immediately. Traffic cops bother me. The possibility of an accident terrifies me. I need to take the car on to a quiet road and learn to handle it confidently again.

The second thing was almost as traumatic in a different way. I went to my first dinner party, as an ex-con. A plunge into the social scene makes less of a splash, Christopher seems to think, when the pool is relatively full. In this case there were fewer guests than we expected. Paul and Samantha usually put on a buffet where you can wander around with a drink and mingle, or not mingle, even quietly depart without fuss. Their penthouse can accommodate thirty. Last night there were only eight guests and we sat around an oval table, eyeball to eyeball, very formal, very polite. I was accepted back into the fold, it was hinted kindly, as if I had never been away from it. That I had missed eighteen months of their lives and didn't know what they were talking about most of the time didn't at first occur to them. Annie had had a divorce. Louella had had a miscarriage. I, according to Paul, who by this time was drinking rather too much, had had a miscarriage of justice. This was followed by silence. Everyone looked at me. Christopher reddened and mumbled something that sounded like "Let's not get on to that, shall we?" but was ignored. I fingered my small pearl pendant that was as unobtrusive as the grey silk dress I was wearing and said, as calmly as I could, that given the circumstances the sentence was correct.

Louella, seated next to me and smelling expensively of Givenchy's Ysatis, declared there must be worse experiences. "I mean, gaol isn't what it was, is it?" She was smiling but her eyes, heavily made up with mauve shadow, were cold. "I don't know," I said. "How was it?" Her smile tightened and she shook back her long mane of blonde hair. "Come on, Maeve! When that sort of thing happens you have to be sensible – put everything into perspective and all that. I mean you weren't flogged, or starved, or put into solitary confinement, or anything. I bet you spent hours being psychoanalysed with your feet up in the shrink's office. And don't tell me you didn't have turkey at Christmas and a party. Okay, they were all women and that couldn't have been good, but apart from that nothing awful happened, did it?"

Oh, no, I thought, nothing awful. The thin little prostitute, Deirdre, cut her wrists with a piece of glass, after reading a letter from her ponce. Only the screws knew what was in it. She wasn't found in time.

One of the inadequates – simple-minded to you, Louella – believed she was pregnant after a lesbian relationship and tried

21

to abort something that wasn't there. Not cataclysmic, perhaps. But bad enough. She ruptured her cervix.

And then there were the addicts – a lost bunch of sick kids and older women, too. You should have seen their punctured flesh, Louella, the colour of their skin, the look in their eyes. They'd been on heroin, and were weaned off with Methedrine. Or partially weaned off – who's to know?

And there was screaming sometimes at night. No – not brutality – just a build-up of despair. Women wanting their kids. Their families.

Oh no, Louella, you fat, sleek bitch in your green velvet gown, nothing awful. You would have loved it.

She's waiting for an answer. "Tell me one terrible thing that you could justly complain about in these enlightened times."

"Well," I said, "the toilet paper was rather rough."

During the rather embarrassed laughter that followed I managed to move clumsily so that I tipped over my glass of red wine. It splashed very satisfactorily into her lap.

She knew it was deliberate, of course. "Oh, fuck!" Her eyes blazed at me.

Mine blazed back, but my voice was as sweet as I could make it. "They said that in there, too. But most of the time they were terribly proper."

It was raining when we left the party and as I sat beside Christopher in the car and watched the wipers swishing across the windscreen I tensed up waiting to be lectured. Instead he was angry on my behalf. "I'm sorry you were subjected to that." I told him not to worry. The evening had turned out worse for Louella. "It was a designer dress worth a few hundred quid."

His sympathy for me perceptibly ebbed a little. It's one thing to throw wine at an enemy when you're high on the adrenalin of combat, but afterwards it's uncivilised to gloat.

Christopher, I'm discovering, did a certain amount of prowling around the job market on my behalf while I was inside. The directors of my old firm don't want me back and under the circumstances nobody could accuse them of unfair dismissal. It seems that the other City firms that Christopher is acquainted with on a business level – and in some cases personally – aren't too sold on the idea of employing me either. Their attitudes might change later on, they hint. While I'm waiting couldn't I set up on my own, they suggest? Advise friends how to tackle their income tax returns, help with VAT, etc? This is rubbish, of course. Who would want to share their financial secrets with me? When I worked in the City I was just a signature on a piece of paper. Part of the money machine. Impersonal. And that's the way people like it.

Our own personal finances are sufficiently sound for it not to matter that I don't contribute. Christopher hints that if we want to start a family this could be the time. A definite, enthusiastic statement that this is most certainly the time to start a family might succeed in persuading me. As it is, I just don't know. You don't create a baby because you can't get a job and you've nothing else to do.

Nothing else to do – except think.

Louella was wrong about the psychoanalysis. If there was a shrink there, I didn't see him. I do know there was someone called a counsellor – a euphemism, perhaps. No one ever counselled me. I would have welcomed the confrontation if they had. A spilling-out of a different kind of aggression. This is the way I think – feel – sir, or madam – dig deep for reasons so that I may refute them. I apologise for nothing, except for hurting that man.

Rene was my confidante. Well, maybe that's not the right word. Half the time I don't believe she listened to me. She neither condemned nor approved. With her I didn't have to justify myself in any way. She certainly didn't try to justify herself to me. We were sisters in crime, she said to me once very cheerfully, and so what the hell? During my first weeks inside she steered me along like a St. Bernard pushing a reluctant traveller through a Siberian wasteland. She had been here before and knew the snares and pitfalls. It amused her, I think, to be proprietorial.

My friends, now that I am here at home, are of a different breed. Those that agree with me politically have been keeping their distance. I have tarnished the peace image a little. My one act of violence has been forgiven, they imply, but don't let's be in any hurry, Maeve, to resume where we left off. Come to the meetings again, Maeve dear, one of them said, but only when you feel ready.

In other words when you're controlled. Sane. Normal.

And my other friends, the ones I used to play squash with, go to the theatre with? Sophie, Malcolm and Jane, Terry? Gone, gone, are the old familiar faces, as the poem said.

And so I'm by myself, as I craved to be when I was inside, and I'm so bloody bored and boring that living with me must be hell.

Christopher is being very patient.

I'll feel better, he says, given time. An unfortunate choice of words. He realises it and smiles at me wryly.

3

I sometimes wonder if Rene and I would have made the effort to get in touch again if we hadn't almost collided with each other outside the Oxford Street store. Probably not. She called the circumstances of our meeting a lucky chance. It was certainly fortuitous for her at that particular moment.

She showed no sign of knowing me when she came briskly out of the shop, and had brushed past me before I could say "Hi" or anything else in greeting. She was several steps down the road when a stout woman of about fifty, wearing a brown headscarf and a grey raincoat, who wasn't the dowdy-looking shopper she appeared to be, put her hand on her arm. There was a muttered conversation which I couldn't overhear and Rene was firmly escorted back inside.

The scenario was obvious. If I hadn't become suddenly aware of the extra weight in my shopping bag I might have hung around to see what I could do. Obviously the best thing was to get home. Fast.

The phone was ringing as I stepped through the front door.

Rene sounded very cheerful. "Your Harrods bag contains a dinosaur," she said. "It has an articulated jaw and an articulated tail that wags. When shall I come and collect it?"

"What the heck are you talking about?" Whatever it was I was delighted to hear her. "Are you going to be charged? I think you're crazy! Are you all right?"

She burbled happily. No, she wasn't going to be charged. They'd found nothing on her. She had boldly suggested to the store manager that she should be compensated for the indignity she'd suffered. He had apologised.

It occurred to me that she had set me up as an accomplice. Used me. I said so, but without rancour.

"Oh, I would have owned up, had the old bitch noticed," she soothed. "I wouldn't have landed you in anything, Maeve. You just happened to be there."

And that's how life moves along, I suppose. Sometimes it gathers momentum and moves out of control. At that particular time I was glad to let it. Rene was better than Valium, or hitting the bottle. She had given me the emotional lift I needed. But a dinosaur?

She arranged to come up to my home and have a bite to eat the following day. Christopher lunched in town and needn't be told.

The dinosaur, complete with battery, cost seventeen pounds, I discovered. It was cute. I played with it on the kitchen table until I heard Christopher's car coming up the drive, then pushed it into the shoe cupboard and went to greet him, smiling.

He was mildly surprised. "Anything up?"

"What do you mean?"

"You're looking happy."

It sounded sarcastic, but wasn't intended that way.

Prison is a leveller. You're all on common ground. It's afterwards that the cracks begin to form, and get wider if you let them. I had looked forward enormously to seeing Rene again but we would have done better to have met for a ploughman's and a lager at the local instead of lunching here at my home. To start with she had difficulty in finding it. Beeches Avenue is a ten minute walk from the bus stop, but she'd got off at the wrong stop. Forty minutes later than I expected her I went to greet her as she toiled up the drive looking hot and rather cross.

"Bloody one-man buses," she complained. "Nobody tells you

anything. I hope you've got stew or something that doesn't spoil."

I told her it was a cold lunch. Smoked salmon and salad.

"So this is executive land," she glanced across the lawn. "At least you can't see your neighbour's washing."

"If it's dirty enough," I said, "it's seen from miles around. Mine's still talked about."

It took her a few seconds to realise I wasn't talking literally.

She needed to go to the loo and I took her up to the bathroom rather than to the cloakroom off the hall. The cloakroom might have been better. Too large a gulp of my rather pretentious home is hard to digest. She eyed the fancy gold taps and the soap resting fatuously on a crystal swan, but didn't comment. "Not my taste," I apologised. "Fixtures and fittings came with the house."

When she joined me ten minutes later I was in the kitchen mopping up the French dressing I'd managed to knock over.

She helped me mop.

Rene has emotional antennae. In prison I knocked things over in times of stress. Which was often. My anxiety now must have puzzled her. I wanted this meeting to work. Why it should matter so much to me, I don't know. Perhaps because I'd been left high and dry by everyone else. There just wasn't anyone to talk to. I had always been able to talk to her. But today it wasn't easy.

She handed the floor cloth back to me.

"It's all right, isn't it?" she asked.

What? The cleaned-up mess? The uneasy re-starting of a friend-ship?

"Fine," I said vaguely, "everything's fine."

She shrugged. "Can I help you carry anything, or do we eat in here?"

I'd laid the table in the conservatory rather than the dining room. Today the sun was pouring in. "If it's not too bright for you, in there."

"Oh my," she said, following me, "pretty super – this." I didn't know if she was referring to the wicker furniture or the view of the orchard.

I told her that Christopher and I had most of our meals in here in the summer, unless we had guests or it was pouring with rain. "It's cosy for two."

"Are you and Christopher cosy?"

Coming from anyone else I would have resented the question – taken it on a deeper level than it was intended. Rene had never done any deep digging. It was probably just a flip rejoinder. Even so, I answered seriously and with a quote from him. "One needs to adjust. It takes a little while."

She gave me a long thoughtful look.

For her, I imagine it had taken no time at all. One, two, three, click. Back in the warm, tumbled, marital bed. Nothing faked. Total acceptance on both sides. Wonderful.

I asked how Oliver was.

"All right. Out of a job at the moment, but that's nothing new."

"What's his line?" It sounded like the quiz game. "I mean, what's he trained for?"

She looked doubtfully at the smoked salmon and tentatively squeezed lemon on it before helping herself to salad. "Pretty well everything that doesn't need training for. Oddjobbing. What does your Christopher do?"

It occurred to me that in the long months we'd known each other this personal background to our lives had never been explored. Our men were unavailable and unimportant, roaming their own territory while we endured ours.

Stockbroking and oddjobbing were too different to be able to speak about with any ease – at least not yet. Later, when we got back on the old footing, that sort of nonsense wouldn't matter. I said he sold things.

"What sort of things?"

"Stocks – shares – bonds."

"You mean money."

"Yes, other people's." I said it was too complicated to explain – that I was vague about it myself.

"But you're an accountant," she persisted.

"Not any more," I told her. "No one will have me."

"Nor me," she said companionably. "Tough, isn't it?"

Tough, the way she said it, could be translated as 'amusing'. Well – amusing when applied to me. Rene's common sense tended

28

to have a sandpaper quality. First it rubbed you raw. I waited for the smoothing-over stage. It came after lunch was over and she'd helped me wash up. We took coffee through to the sitting room – her suggestion. "I want to see the rest of your place."

She examined the room, much as I had on my first day out of prison in February. "So," she said at last, "this is you."

I was on the defensive. "No more than your place is you."

"Which is a hell of a lot of me. And most of me I can't help."

"Any more than I can."

"Don't kid yourself." She squatted down, her back to the sofa, and ran her hands over the design of the Chinese rug. "You've got it all, Maeve. So what's bugging you?"

She wanted to know so I tried to tell her. Prison had knocked me sideways. Nobody could imagine it, who had never been inside. Only she could understand what I meant. She had been kind to me in there. I could tell her my nightmares. I still had them. "In your case," I finished, "you didn't hurt anybody. At least, not physically."

She shrugged. "You could have run that copper over with a car. Just as much an accident. How would you feel about that?"

"That's not relevant. It didn't happen that way."

"Well," she said, "you didn't plan anything. Not like me."

Rene's planned criminal activities had never at any stage shocked me. When I was inside with her I was too stunned by what I'd done to Sergeant Sutherland to judge morally what I saw as a much more minor offence. She stole. I maimed. I would have swopped her crime and her conscience with mine, any day.

And I still, as I spoke to her, felt the same.

"The trouble with you," Rene said, "is you're an idealist." This was so completely off beam, and sounded so extraordinary coming from her, that it silenced me utterly.

Taking the subject as closed, Rene suggested that I should fetch Wayne's toy. "And then I've got to get back to him."

"Wayne?"

"My kid."

"I didn't know you . . ."

She cut in. "That I have a son? Well, I have. He's four. I didn't blab too much about him when I was in stir, in case the Social

29

Services got their hands on him. If you'd had a kid I expect one of your posh relatives would have looked after him."

She stood up and glanced around the room once more. "Arrangements," she said, "would have been made. You don't know how bloody lucky you are, Maeve. You really don't."

"Material possessions," I told her bleakly, "aren't everything."

She gave me a crooked little smile and didn't answer.

I offered to drive her home, rather hoping she wouldn't accept the offer, but she did. I had taken the mini out a few times and was gradually getting more confident with it, but I hadn't driven into the City traffic since Chornley. After crashing the gears a few times and holding the wheel as if it were a lifebuoy in a boiling sea, I gradually calmed down. There weren't cops at every corner ready to book me. The aggressors were the usual ones, cabs and buses. I wished the mini were heavier, more competitive, like the old timer of a Buick that was forging ahead, all glittering chrome and heavy metal. Perhaps I'd buy myself a bigger car, something with more bonnet and taller. I almost said this aloud but stopped myself in time.

If Rene hadn't been guiding me I doubt if I could have found her flat in Hackney. It was in a reclaimed terraced property in a grotty area and the reclamation work was, to put it mildly, skimped. The owner had acquired most of the street, she told me, and the remaining houses in the row were boarded up until more cash was available. When it was, the whole lot would be tarted up and sold to the yuppy brigade who had more money than sense and she and the other folks still there would be out on their bums. She didn't seem too bothered by the prospect, but then she rarely bothered about anything. Potential Rachmanism, if I lived here, wouldn't have bothered me either. The place was not only tatty, it was depressing. I had imagined her living in a council flat, even a run-down one with external corridors and graffiti on the walls. Somewhere throbbing with life. The heart-beat here had the slow tempo of age. It wasn't a Rene environment, just a place she had found and was temporarily putting up with.

"It's not too bad inside," she said, reading my expression before I could control it. "Ours is the first floor flat."

The flats weren't custom-built and the downstairs hallway was shared. Two nameplates by the front door were situated beside two bells, and a smudged card indicated that Flat Two was the Dudgeons'. The name beside Flat One was such a scrawl I couldn't read it. "Old Ma' Heaton's," Rene said, noticing my squinting at it. "She keeps an eye on Wayne. I buy her oranges."

This seemed an odd payment for neighbourly favours. Over in my own world, on the other side of the divide, it's flowers, chocolates or a bottle of good wine . . . Oranges? Well, why not?

"She gets through half a dozen a day," Rene explained. "Needs vitamin C – or something. Expensive."

Practical Rene. I imagined her walking through the market, nicking oranges from the stalls.

We went upstairs and she ushered me in with a crisp "Well, here it is. Don't blame Olly or me for the wallpaper. We didn't choose it."

It was red flock on a beige background, thick enough to hold cracks together without disguising them. "If it were mine," I said unwisely, "I'd emulsion it white."

"If it was yours," she replied rather sharply, "I'm quite sure you would. But aren't you glad it's not?"

I had shared a similar flat with a couple of students when I was studying at the LSE. That had been worse. We had, however, made it better.

In prison Rene had made her room better. She had prettied it up. I was the one who hadn't bothered. A cell was a cell. Sticking calendar pictures on the walls of cute little dogs and cats and idyllic country scenes didn't alter the fact. When I'd told her this she hadn't argued, just pointed out placidly that as erotic male pin-ups were hard to come by you had to do the best you could. "Or nothing," she had added, "if that's the way it takes you."

It's a philosophy of acceptance. That was why she had weathered prison so well. The chaplain had preached a sermon one Sunday about kicking against the pricks – or rather, *not* kicking – which had aroused some ribaldry afterwards – but Rene had taken it as it had been intended, and thoroughly approved.

"In any case," she went on now, "Why bother? Why spend money on someone else's property?"

31

The main living room overlooked a small back garden, where weeds pushed up between paving stones. A powerful motorbike was parked next to a child's red tricycle just inside the back gate.

I asked where father and son were.

"Oh, around – " Rene said vaguely. "Off somewhere in the van, if he's had it fixed. A new clutch plate or something."

She showed me the rest of the flat – a fairly large double bedroom – same wallpaper – a double bed neatly made. And next to it the child's room, filled with expensive toys. Wayne, quite obviously, didn't want for anything. Rene put the dinosaur on his Pinocchio bedspread. "A surprise for tonight. He needs a bit of spoiling. He's had a rough time."

I was curious about the child, but she changed the subject abruptly. "I've had a new microwave. Come and see it."

I followed her to the kitchen. The microwave oven, quite a large one, took up most of the space on top of a rickety table. "I've no room for it. Do you want to buy it, or have you already got one? Olly acquired it yesterday."

Acquired is a flexible word. Not exact. I wondered if it had fallen off the back of a lorry.

"It was given to him," Rene said, reading my expression, "by a friend."

I blushed.

She laughed. "Oh, Maeve, Maeve, how the sweet hell did I put up with you all those bloody months! If I wanted to flog stolen property I wouldn't flog it to you. We're mates, aren't we – for Christ's sake?"

We were, in that moment, mates again.

I told her I had one. She replied equably, "Of course."

My first impression of Oliver outside the prison had been fleeting – and totally wrong. No Ford Madox Brown emigrant type came bounding up the stairs into the flat half an hour after Rene and I had settled down with a cup of tea. His face and hands were streaked with oil, apparently he'd been working under the van himself, and the little boy riding his shoulders was filthy.

They were both laughing as they came in. Laughter that stopped when they saw me.

"Oh," Oliver said.

Rene made protesting sounds about the child's condition. "Where have you been? You've oil all over you. You never took him to the garage with you? You both stink!"

She helped him slide off and he disappeared behind his father, clutching his jeans.

Rene softened her voice. "Okay, kiddo. I'm not cross. Come on, then, come and meet Maeve."

He stayed where he was, eyeing me with deep suspicion.

Oliver, more concerned with the child's reaction than the reason for it, mouthed at Rene not to fuss. "Give him time."

This, I sensed, shocked, wasn't just a child who was shy with strangers, as many children are, this was a child who had been traumatised.

His parents coaxed him as they would a little frightened animal so that he advanced further into the room. Rene quietly closed the outer door. He noticed. Whimpered.

Dear God, I thought, what happened to him, when his mother was inside? Who hurt him?

The bedroom door was ajar and I noticed the dinosaur in its box on the bed. It might divert his attention, or would it frighten him more?

I got up quietly, fetched it, and sat with the box on my knee. To open it or not? I didn't know.

"Oh, great!" Rene's voice was artificially cheerful. "Maeve's present. Look what Maeve's brought you. Isn't it smashing?"

She squatted down beside me and took the dinosaur out of the box. Oliver joined us. He wound it up and the three of us played with it with apparent absorption while the little boy watched. He had the same colouring as Rene, but his red hair was thin and straight. His eyes, dark brown, partially veiled by eyelashes fairer than his hair, were wary.

He wanted to approach the toy, but while I was there he wouldn't.

I stood up and murmured quietly that I'd better be off. That I'd see them again sometime.

Rene, obviously relieved, didn't try to detain me. "Well, thanks for buying him the present. Next time you come just bring your-self. No need for gifts. Lovely to see you."

There was a message in her voice and in her eyes. *Gift*, it stressed. *Yours*. I didn't nick it. You bought it. Very legit. Okay?

She told her son to wave goodbye. He stared at me like a cold little statue, unmoving.

Oliver came over to the door with me. "I'll see you down to your car. I suppose the white mini is yours?"

"Yes, but don't leave the little boy. I'll see myself out."

"No trouble. Anyway, my van's parked rather close. I'll move it."

His van was blue and rusting and as dirty as he was. He drove it forward and then came back to me with a piece of clean sacking over his arm. "If I put this on the seat can I sit with you for a minute or two? I won't muck up the upholstery."

"Of course," I opened the front passenger door for him.

We were both speaking in our normal voices now, the rather hushed more gentle tones not needed any more. His accent was northern, I thought, from somewhere near the Scottish border. A contrast to Rene's Cockney.

He must have been listening to mine. "So this is Irish Maeve. The lady with the brick." He sounded amused, not censorious.

I explained that my father had been a general practitioner in Langdon, the village where they'd buried the nuclear waste, and that he'd died a few years ago. "He was on the side of the healers, not the destroyers. He would have approved of my protest, but not of the violence. I hadn't intended that." I added, "Yes, he was Irish. His accent was slight: I hadn't realised I'd inherited it."

He didn't answer and I guessed that he wasn't sitting beside me now because he wanted to discuss accents – or bricks. He wanted to discuss matters more personal to him.

He led up to what he had to say. "Rene tells me you were a good pal to her in Chornley."

I told him bleakly that she had been kind to me – had helped me to survive it.

"The people outside have to survive, too," he said. "Especially the kids. If Rene is pushed into the slammer again, she'll lose Wayne. He's emotionally unstuck – you've seen that for yourself. We're trying to get him together again. You understand me?"

"Yes, I do. He's a great kid. It's obvious you both love

34

him . . . I . . ." I felt awash with embarrassment and couldn't go on. He was about to ask me if Rene had nicked the dinosaur and I was about to lie on her behalf and say no. I don't usually lie. I'm no good at it. Anyway, he knows damned well she nicked it. She's not all that brilliant a liar herself. Her performance just now was pathetic. I understand his anxiety.

He's looking at me closely and he doesn't ask the question. "All right," he says, "ease up. Not your problem."

He gets out of the car. "Did Rene try to sell you the micro-wave?"

"She showed it to me. I have one."

"Oh, well – if you want any other consumer durables at cut price just ask. I have contacts."

"I'll remember."

"Good," he says, "good." And then he smiles.

I like him. He's probably as crooked as Rene. But it doesn't matter. It should, but it doesn't. I like them both.

"Some," he says, "get bothered about the big issues. Our nuclear winters – Rene's and mine – are leaking pipes and no central heating. Small matters. Next time there's a local riot, come and throw a brick for us."

He laughs. I can't join in, but I'm not offended. It's a point of view.

4

The BBC have contacted me. Radio Four are doing a series
called *Reactions*. Reaction to bereavement. To divorce. To
bankruptcy. To prison. A more up-beat series is apparently being
planned, but that's for later. In this first series they are interested
in women who can articulate their experiences, and they would
appreciate my taking part. As I was released from the Open
Prison three months ago, they go on, I might be able to view
the experience more objectively than if they had made the request
earlier. The broadcast would be recorded within the next couple
of weeks and at a mutually convenient date. If I agree.

The letter arrived at breakfast time and I passed it to Christopher.
My mail, good, bad and indifferent, had trickled down to nothing
and this took me by surprise. My first reaction was: no.

Christopher read it, frowning. "Absolutely not," he said.
"You're out of the public eye, becoming more normal: I won't
allow you to be the focus of attention again."

"Becoming more normal?"

He handed the letter back to me. "More like yourself. You
know what I mean. Write them a refusal and then tear this up."

"More like myself?"

Christopher is not a morning person. His irritability bubbles like a pan on the boil until he's had his elevenses at the office. He might have used more tact had the day been further advanced.

"More like yourself when you're in a reasonable frame of mind. Don't start an argument about semantics, for God's sake."

"I don't like woolly expressions that don't mean anything. Any more than I like sentences such as . . ." I refer to the letter, 'women who can articulate their experiences' instead of 'women who can talk about what happened to them.'"

"Good," he said, relaxing a little, "then write and tell what's-hisname – the programme director – in words of one syllable that you won't go."

"You seem very certain I shouldn't."

"You surely don't want to?"

I hadn't until that moment wanted to. "I need time to think about it."

"That's your trouble," Christopher said, "too much time. And I don't know how you use it."

I wondered if he was referring to the state of the house – the infrequent hoovering – the sketchy dusting – and the meals that were less than brilliant. The daily help had left just before I came out of prison and I still felt too raw to have anyone else around.

"One of these days," I told him, "we'll have a dinner party. I'll make the effort. Friends will re-appear. All will be well."

He pushed his coffee cup aside and looked at me critically. "You could start by getting dressed in the morning."

"My dressing-gown annoys you?"

"Your dressing-gown mentality. Get off your sick bed, Maeve. Your period of convalescence is lasting too long. Show some spirit. You're a woman of intelligence. Start living your life again as it should be lived."

As you would have me live it, I thought. But there was sense in what he said. I had done a lot of cowering behind doors: it was time to open a few and step outside. I decided in that moment to do the interview, but it wasn't the time to tell him.

In retrospect I realise that my reason for agreeing to be interviewed is more complex than it seems. Masochism. Guilt. Bravado. They are part of it, but the despairing recurrent nightmare about Sutherland is the strongest motive.

In my dream the crowds have gone, and he is walking towards me across a dark field. Soft footsteps on grass. A starless sky. I walk towards him and we seem to merge so that the blood on his face streaks my cheeks like tears. I awake crying, but silently into the pillow so that Christopher doesn't hear.

My sense tells me that the great big listening world out there won't offer absolution for anything I might say during a radio interview. I said very little during my trial: I was too shocked and the judge was repressive. But I have a stronger voice now, and a chance to use it. Some might understand. Even Sutherland himself. In a way it's a reaching-out to him.

Christopher, fuming, insists on coming to the broadcasting studio with me. He had used every ploy he could think of to dissuade me and, failing, has set himself up as an aggressive watch-dog.

He tells the interviewer, Simon Macbarra, immediately after we are introduced to him, that he strongly disapproves. "There could be unpleasant repercussions. My wife has been hurt enough."

I am used to Christopher talking for me. It is annoying, but that's his nature. The ten-year gap in our ages has made him paternalistic. I suppose that's why I do my fair share of shouting on my own behalf.

I tell Macbarra, who is looking nonplussed, that we haven't come to call off the interview, we've come because I intend doing it.

He is relieved and offers coffee.

This is followed by a softening-up chat. The soothing of the interviewee's nerves, I guess. And in this case, the placating of Christopher.

Macbarra explains that he and I will chat casually and easily for about half an hour or so, but that the actual transmission will last half that time. "There will be careful editing," he reassures Christopher. "If Mrs. Barclay says anything unwise – anything she might later regret – that part will be wiped off the tape. There's nothing to worry about."

I wish he would address these remarks to me.

Christopher asks if he may be allowed to sit in the transmitting studio, or whatever it's called, with me. Macbarra says no, but that there's no objection to his sitting in the adjoining room where he can see me through the glass partition and hear what is being said.

There are shades of prison supervision about all this. I don't know whether to be amused or angry. My nerves are beginning to tighten.

Macbarra is thirty-ish. Small, fair and with long humorous lips that quirk at me with a degree of sympathy as he takes me into the room where the mike is. "Honestly," he says, "it will be all right."

"I hope so." I'm not so sure now that it will be.

The mike is on the table, and looks like a small hand-grenade on a stick. When I imagined all this, I imagined it differently. Old-fashioned headphones – a voice at a distance – an anonymous interrogation. There are such places as single studios, I believe. You can remove the headphones at any stage and walk out.

I want to walk out now.

Christopher, seated by another man beside another gadget, is looking at me through the glass. He is willing me to walk out now, too.

I raise my hand in an airy gesture of confidence I don't feel and smile at him. He frowns.

Macbarra goes into a few technical details. When the red light goes on he wants me to speak a few words into the mike, to get the sound level right, and after that we'll get on with the actual interview. "Before we do, are there any areas you want to avoid?"

I tell him my mind is blank. I can't think of any.

He smiles his long thin-lipped smile, which is somehow warming, and says once again that everything is okay – not to worry.

The red light goes on. I count aloud from one to ten. Macbarra moves the mike back a little way. "Just sit comfortably. That's about the right distance. Fine."

He has a page of notes in front of him and uses them for the introductory opening which gives details of what he calls 'the offence', where and when it happened, the length of the sentence and the date of release. It's very cool and impersonal. I feel as if he's talking about someone else. He has bony wrists, I notice, and wears a signet ring on his little finger.

I become aware that he is regarding me and has put the notes aside.

"And now that I have filled you in with the background," he says, "let me tell you a little about the lady herself. When Mrs. Barclay agreed to come here today, agreed to re-live what must have been quite a harrowing experience, I had no preconceived idea of what to expect. Now that she is sitting here in the studio, across the table from me, I see an attractive woman in her middle twenties. She is quietly dressed in a plum coloured corduroy suit with matching shoes. Her light brown hair, casually styled in a long bob, frames her pale, sensitive face. But am I right in using the adjective sensitive? Would a sensitive woman have acted as she did? And if so, how would she have reacted to the consequences?"

He pauses, "Mrs. Barclay . . . may I call you Maeve . . .? I'd like to put those questions to you. What motivated you to act so violently at Langdon – and afterwards could you justify to yourself what you had done?"

Macbarra, I realise, is a smiling enemy. The knowledge stiffens me.

I have to answer, and I do. Calmly.

"There is no justification for violence. Of any kind. There was never any intention that the protest at Langdon should develop as it did. It started peacefully and should have continued that way. The villagers were protecting their heritage from nuclear pollution – the burying of radioactive waste on land that was too close to them. They were concerned for themselves – their children – the future generations. It was when the excavators tried to drive through our ranks that the rabble fringe moved in. They're at most demonstrations. Stones and bricks began to be thrown. One grazed my arm. I picked it up and threw it back. Impulsively. Stupidly. If I had a target at all, it certainly wasn't Sutherland."

"Sutherland. The police sergeant you injured."

It is a statement not requiring an answer, but I nod silently. "I would give ten years of my life for it not to have happened."

I want to say more. I have come here to say more, but the words won't form.

"Instead," Macbarra continues smoothly, "you gave eighteen months of your life – in prison. And that's what we're here to talk about." He glances at his notes. "You spent the first few weeks in Holloway. For a woman of your background you must have found that very difficult."

"Any woman would find it difficult."

"Yes, obviously, but you, perhaps, more than most. You had been gently nurtured, to use an old-fashioned phrase. A comfortable home background. Public school education. A professional life with intellectual peers. To be thrust amongst the criminal class must be quite a shock."

I think about Rene and am silent.

He persists. "Or did your earlier confrontations at Greenham Common prepare you to some extent?"

I am stung into a response. "I was fined for cutting the wire on the perimeter fence. There was no violence . . . by any of us."

"I wasn't suggesting . . ."

"As for 'criminal class' – how do you see the women in Holloway – in other prisons? As a distinct breed? If so, in what way do I escape the classification? I don't, of course. How could I?"

He says quietly, rather amused. "Calm it – you'll give your husband a heart attack." The red light goes out and we are temporarily off the air. I avoid looking through the glass partition at Christopher.

Macbarra offers me a cigarette. I refuse. He lights up.

"Mrs. Barclay . . . Maeve . . . I'm not being intentionally abrasive, it's just that I want a response." He qualifies it, "A controlled response. I've a feeling that you might like a political platform and I'd probably sympathise with a lot of your views, but this isn't the place for it. I want to know how you reacted to prison. 'Criminal class' was a perfectly valid way of expressing it, but if you think I'm being a moral snob then I retract it. I'm quite sure you were given a custodial sentence for something that was just bad luck, and that you were probably a victim of prejudice. I can't say that in the broadcast, though.

41

This is supposed to be unbiased reporting. So shall we press on?"

"That's what I'm here for."

"Quite. So okay for more action?"

The red light comes on again.

He rephrases what he has said earlier. "To be suddenly thrust into such an alien atmosphere must have been quite a shock. How did you cope?"

"By closing off part of my mind. Accepting what had to be accepted."

"Can you expand that?"

I can, but I won't. The first few days were the most shocking. The claustrophobic horror of being locked in. The strip search, dignity discarded like the clothes I was told to take off. The prison bath with no privacy. The medical examination by a doctor who was probably checking for drugs and VD. All of this left me shaken and sick. For a while I couldn't bear to look at myself in a mirror. I despised what I saw. I had become a number. One of a herd. Processed. Raw, vulnerable, shamed. I refuse to expose my shame to the listening world out there and instead mumble something about the cold.

"You mean physical cold – or the coldness of an inimical atmosphere?"

'Inimical atmosphere' will do. It's near enough.

"I managed to adjust," I lie, avoiding the question. "Afterwards, when I was moved to the Open Prison, it was easier."

"Chornley is one of the newer prisons, I believe. How would you describe it?"

An institution made pretty with curtains at the windows, a crèche for babies, association rooms with carpeted floors and prints of rural scenes on the walls. All true. Is that what he wants me to say? It is, of course, so I say it.

"A pleasant enough background," he observes.

I have a sudden vivid memory of my grandmother, whom I'd loved very much, lying in her white silk padded coffin. That had been pretty, too. It hadn't stopped her looking dead.

He asks about the screws. "How did you react to the prison officers? Did you find it difficult to take orders from them?"

You go into prison expecting to take orders. If you're wheeled into hospital, obeying orders is part of survival. You don't tell the doctors what to do. It isn't your body any more. It's on loan to the system. The new screws who tried to fraternise too much were worse than the experienced ones who made the demarcation line clear. You knew where you stood with the old hands: *just toe the line, Maeve, function as you're told, and don't think.*

I answer truthfully, after a short pause, that most of the orders were reasonable. "There had to be rules. I understood that."

"Were you addressed by your surname?"

"No. The officers used our Christian names. And they were Mrs. or Miss Whatever, when we spoke to them."

"It sounds like a boarding school environment. Was that how it seemed to you?"

"No."

In a boarding school you're paying to be there – or rather your family is. You're not expected to go down on your knees and scrub floors. Or peel potatoes in the kitchen. Domestic chores aren't part of the curriculum. If you misbehave you're expelled, not made to stay longer. You may hate your boarding school, but you're not ashamed of it, and most of the time it doesn't shame you.

Macbarra waits, wanting more. I tell him it's a prison and can't be compared with anything else.

"Were all the staff women?"

"Yes, apart from the ancillary staff. They seemed to be able to cope, even when things got rough."

"Rough?"

Yes, Macbarra. *Rough.* Screws have been roughed up – badly. The job is no sinecure. And cons have attacked other cons – almost killed them.

"An upsurge of animosity now and then," I tell him. "Women with different temperaments forced to live together. Arguments weren't always polite."

He gets the picture. "Were you subjected to physical abuse at any time?"

A woman called Marge backhanded me across the face once for no particular reason. She'd just spent a few days in 'strips', the cell that's bare of everything except a mattress, for being truly violent to somebody else. Slapping me was probably the last surge of anger before a period of calm.

"No," I tell Macbarra, "never." A slap doesn't count.

"Mental cruelty?"

I think about that before answering. "Cruelty is a subjective concept. We are all of us cruel to each other sometimes. Not always intentionally."

He looks at me quizzically, aware perhaps that the glossing over with fancy words conceals a non-reply. Anyway, I can't, won't, be more specific.

He doesn't pursue it. "Would you agree that prison these days has a constructive role to play in the rehabilitation of prisoners, especially those going out into the world again after long sentences?"

"Perhaps. It didn't apply in my case. My sentence was comparatively short."

"What about education – preparation for jobs – careers, and so on?"

"There were classes graded according to ability. Some cons learnt to read. Others studied for university entrance."

And a lot of cons learnt a few more anti-social skills to add to the ones they already had, but you're not a fool, Macbarra, and neither are the people out there listening, so I'm not underlining what you already know.

He asks how I spent the association period. "In the library, perhaps, or the art room?"

I had spent it with Rene in any quiet corner we could find, and she'd taught me to knit. I had made half a jumper, red with black diamonds on it. She had finished it. As far as I know she still has it.

Rene. Reality. My control begins to slip. "Oh yes," I say, "the library and the art room." Two civilised areas constantly referred to. I remember my conversation with Louella and nearly invent something about sitting in with the shrink. That, however, might have repercussions.

If anyone had needed analysis it was Anna. She spent most of her free time painting the same picture over and over in monochrome. Rolling moorland, a small house in the distance. Sometimes the scene was red so that the moorland looked like blood. Often it was shades of grey like oncoming night. Rene used to tease her about them, call them fodder for the shrink, and she'd look at her sombre-eyed and say nothing. Her pictures gave me the creeps and it worries me, even now, to think of them.

"Painting pictures," I tell him, "is therapeutic. So they say. You slosh the paint around. Violence exploding harmlessly on to canvas. Great blobs of carmine. That sort of thing."

But Anna hadn't sloshed it around. She had been neat and careful. The blue apron she had worn over her dress, not a smock, more the kind you wear in a hairdresser's, had been unmarked. What bothered me was the smallness of the house, drawn first and with meticulous detail, compared with the encroaching moorland which seemed about to smother it with grass. Had her home meant that much to her – or that little? What had happened there? What, for God's sake, had she done? I'd asked Rene and she'd shrugged and not answered. She probably didn't know. It was usually better not to.

I notice that Macbarra is glancing towards the window dividing the two rooms and making a reassuring face at Christopher. That last bit about violence will, I guess, be deleted.

He turns back to me. "Are you bitter about your experience, Maeve?"

Obviously I'm bitter. It's obvious to him and, only just now, obvious to me. Prison, I believed, had been necessary to cauterise my guilt. I still believe it, but I *am* bitter and the cauterising hasn't worked. Hasn't worked enough. Guilt doesn't heal that easily, no matter what you do. Perhaps it never heals.

"I have no reason to be bitter," I tell him, "but reason doesn't come into it, does it?"

I'm beginning to feel very tired. The room is hot and I can feel a trickle of sweat worming down my spine.

He becomes aware of my discomfort and stops the recording for a couple of minutes. "You're doing fine. We're nearly there." He pours me some water from a carafe on the table. It's tepid, but I drink it dutifully.

"Okay again?" He's smiling.

I nod. We carry on.

"You must have rubbed shoulders with many quite vicious inmates, before you were transferred to the Open Prison. How did you react on a personal level? To child killers, for instance?"

I tell him that child killers were kept apart. "They were isolated for their own safety. Other murderers mingled with the rest of us." Sadie, a gently-spoken, elderly woman, had shocked me one day by telling me graphically how she had slit her husband's throat. It's the kind of story that Macbarra and the radio fans would like to hear. But they won't hear it from me.

He seems to read my mind. "At times you must have heard things that appalled you."

"Yes."

"Can you expand that?"

"No."

"Why not?"

"They're in there. I'm out here. And it's all a matter of degree. The police sergeant I injured could have died."

"And that weighs very heavily on your conscience. I'm sorry I ever doubted your sensitivity. You are obviously a very caring person."

I don't comment. What he has just said is for the listeners. Caring? I wish to God I didn't care.

"There is a very important question I feel I must ask, though I know in your case it doesn't apply. Do you believe that prison can corrupt?"

"In what way?"

He folds up his notes carefully so that the papers don't rustle near the mike and puts them neatly beside the carafe. "We hear a lot about violence, read about it, see it on television. We can, to some extent, get used to it. In prison the focus is a lot narrower, a lot sharper. It's a climate of crime. Isn't it easy for some to put aside the moral code, to go along with the crowd?"

Once again I think of Rene. We have become mates, as she said. We accept each other's crimes without condemning. I wouldn't embezzle or shoplift. She wouldn't hurl a brick.

"Is tolerance a polite word for corruption?"

To respond to his question with a question isn't on. He shakes his head at me. "I'm asking you. What do you think?"

"There's a lot of pain," I point out, "and frustration. Everywhere. There is no special breeding ground for corruption. Prison will corrupt some. Social injustice outside will corrupt others. People climb on each other's backs for lots of reasons, then push them under. When the big City boys make a few millions by bending the rules they're not always slammed inside. When a young mum squeezes an illicit few hundred out of Social Security she gets eighteen months." (And when she gets out she shoplifts a dinosaur, I think. Incorrigible Rene. But corrupt? Corrupting?)

Macbarra is smiling at me. I'm on my soap box again and the red light is out. "Go on," he says pleasantly, "no one is listening. Not even your worried husband."

I find I have nothing else to say. This broadcast was probably a mistake. I want to end it. And tell him.

He doesn't argue. There is sufficient material, he says, to make it worthwhile.

5

"If that was supposed to be cathartic, then I hope you're feeling better," Christopher grumbled at me over a hurried lunch, afterwards. His face was drawn into deep lines of annoyance. Macbarra had taken him aside after the interview, but whatever soothing remarks had been made, they hadn't made him any happier.

"It has always seemed odd," he went on caustically, "that you can speak more easily to other people than to me. Why spill out all that grief to a stranger – and to God knows how many people who'll tune in?"

That was unanswerable. I pushed the pizza around on my plate. Not hungry.

"Or were you trying to get to Sutherland?" he probed with uncanny accuracy. "A public *mea culpa*? Was that what it was all about?"

I had never told him about my nightmares, and was half tempted to tell him now. But the restaurant was crowded. There was a queue at the door. The waitress was hovering.

"If you feel you must salve your conscience," he went on, obviously not expecting an answer, "why don't you get involved in Good Works in some benign form? For God's sake, Maeve, it's the ordinary people doing ordinary things to help other people that make life easier."

He was right, of course. He always is.

He had to go back to his office to make life easier for his rich clients.

I decided to make life easier for Rene.

Buying a new outfit for Wayne seemed the best way of setting about it. I chose to shop in a store that specialised in childrens' clothes and the assistant was helpful. "A little boy of four," I told her. "Red-haired. Rather frail."

It was after she had selected a bright assortment of pants and jerseys for me to see that I realised they wouldn't fit. He was taller than the average child of four and the five to six sizes looked more like him. Oliver was tall; obviously he was taking after him. I told the assistant and she agreed that children varied in their rate of development, that sizes were approximate, and that it was better to choose something too big than too small. And so we started again. Kids' clothes are fun. He'd love the pyjamas with pictures of trains on the front and I found a matching dressing-gown and added it to the pile of clothes on the counter. It was nice to be choosing for Wayne, it would have been even nicer had I been choosing for a child of my own and for a while I dreamed I was. It was a natural feminine reaction perhaps to a shop that titillated the maternal instinct.

Wayne's clothes added up to quite a lot. The assistant removed the price tags and parcelled them while I wrote a cheque. Rene, with the essentials supplied, would have cash in hand now to buy her child a toy and not nick it. Or so I told myself. I suppose we always try to justify our actions when we're not quite sure of them.

It wasn't easy to justify them to Oliver. He came on his motorbike on Wednesday afternoon when Walker should have been there cutting the grass. Walker had sent a note to say he was sick and wouldn't be able to come for a while, and I was clumsily guiding the machine around myself. Oliver must have been watching me for a couple of minutes before I saw him and

49

switched the mower off. He had a plastic bag in his hand and didn't look pleased.

The day was blustery and grass had blown everywhere. I tried to brush it off the front of my jeans and left green streaks. The air smelt of petrol from his machine.

"I took a chance on barging in on you," he said, "to return these."

I had packed Wayne's clothes in brown paper and sent them anonymously. The plastic bag advertised a supermarket. To gain time I tried to look mystified. "To return what?"

"You know what. I don't want you spending your money on us. Anything my family wants I get for them."

"Yes," I said, "of course. I'm sorry."

He handed the bag to me. I took it, embarrassed. A sleeve of the pyjama jacket hung a little way out of the bag. I tucked it back in.

My mother would call an occasion like this a social *faux pas*. They tend to occur to her class-conscious generation. Not to mine. I had belittled Oliver – unintentionally – been crassly insensitive.

He could see I was upset. "You meant it kindly," his voice was rather less metallic now, the razored tones blunted a little, "but we don't take charity from our friends."

"No." I wasn't looking at him. It was easier to keep my gaze fixed on the piece of rose trellis that was swaying in the wind and needed hammering back.

The silence grew. Awkwardly.

He broke it. "You've grass in your hair." He touched my hair briefly. "Just there. The machine should have a box on it."

I drew my hand across my temple. Where he had touched. Not much grass. Not worth mentioning.

"I suppose you rake it up afterwards?"

Banal subject – grass. "The man who cuts it does. He couldn't come."

"And your trellis has worked loose."

"He would have done that, too."

"Maeve – look at me."

I look.

"Do you want to kick me out for being an ungrateful bastard – or do you want me to stay and mow your lawn?"

50

He's not smiling, but the anger has gone. His embarrassment now equals mine. We both need to make amends.

While Oliver cut the lawn I put Wayne's clothes in an old suitcase on top of the wardrobe and then went down to make him a cup of tea. A reflex action. I had always brewed up for Walker and taken the tray out to the summerhouse, as he refused to drink it in the kitchen. "People would talk," he told me on a dark drizzly day when I had tried to persuade him to come indoors. As he was approaching sixty and hardly a sex object I had found this funny. So had Christopher when I told him.

Christopher wouldn't find anything remotely amusing about Oliver.

He came to the kitchen door. "I need a hammer and nails – for the trellis."

He had taken off his motorcycling jacket and wore a white tee shirt with Le Mans printed on it in black. He had narrow well-shaped hands, I noticed, but his arms were strongly muscled. He and Rene would probably be very good in bed together.

"For the trellis," he repeated, "I want to put it back up."

"Won't you have some tea first?" I sounded like a dowager, but didn't feel like one.

He said he'd have a drink of something – preferably not tea – after he'd seen to the trellis. I went to the tool shed with him and stayed around handing up the nails while he hammered.

Preferably not tea left him a choice of coffee – wine – spirits – or lager. He chose a can of lager and drank it standing up in the conservatory where Rene and I had had lunch.

"Rene said you had a nice place," he said, "It is. Very."

I had a feeling he was tailoring his words to fit the environment – I had been *kindly* – my home was *nice*. (Let's have a nice, dull conversation, Oliver, and then you must go.)

"But your security system is rotten," he went on. "Anyone could break in."

Not dull – but not menacing, either.

I pointed out that we had a burglar alarm.

He said he'd noticed. "It isn't much good. It'll keep a prowler out. That's all."

"Well," I said, "I suppose that's something."

"It's nothing to joke about."

"I'm not joking."

"But you're not serious: you don't care about things you might prevent, you just get bothered about things you can't."

He's beginning to sound like Christopher. They both tend to harp on the same subject. Oliver's parting words to me at our last meeting had been much the same. If he and Christopher ever got together – which God forbid – at least they'd be in accord on this one issue.

"If you'll fetch me a pencil and paper," he says, "I'll jot down the names of burglar alarms that are better than yours. They're not perfect, none of them are."

I do as he asks. Just to humour him. If Christopher is happy with the security here, then why bother?

Oliver's handwriting is very neat and he draws clear diagrams. I tell him he would be an excellent representative for the firm he's promoting. He says drily that he isn't promoting any firm, he's just helping a friend. This time the word is spoken with warmth.

"If the man who cuts your lawn doesn't come back," he says, "I can take over for a few weeks. If your husband agrees."

The proviso silences me. Of course Christopher wouldn't agree.

"That is, if you want me to," he adds, when I'm slow to answer.

I do want him to, and can't persuade myself otherwise. I tell him that Christopher leaves all domestic arrangements, including the garden, to me. And that I would be very pleased if he came, provided he brings Rene and Wayne along. "Every Wednesday afternoon at two o'clock for a couple of hours, if that's okay? Wayne can play on the lawn and Rene and I can have a good natter."

Oliver gives me a level look. We are beginning to understand one another very well. Barriers all around. All of us safe and good.

There is, however, one delicate matter. If your friend cuts your grass do you slip him a bottle of the best Scotch in payment – or what? I'm still remembering the return of Wayne's clothes.

He seems to sense my dilemma and tells me that he charges the usual hourly rate. I discover that it is slightly higher than the amount I paid Walker, but am happy to agree.

"A fair return for work done," Oliver says, brusque and businesslike.

"Yes," I say. "A good arrangement."

There is a fine line between lying and being economical with the truth. Christopher didn't know that Walker had stopped coming. I hadn't shown him Walker's final note which stated that he was getting too old for the job. If he had asked about him, I would have done. Oliver tended the garden rather better than Walker had. He was particularly good about edging the lawn, but if Christopher noticed he probably thought that Walker was being more attentive than usual.

I was being deceitful, but I couldn't care. I was glad to have my friends around me. You don't know you're lonely until someone fills the void and you realise how nice it is. On Wednesdays the sun shone, or seemed to, most of the time.

It shone particularly brightly for Wayne. He was like a small, shy, forest creature exploring the quiet places in the garden while Oliver did the mowing and edging and Rene and I just sat around or did a little weeding if we felt inclined. The child would watch me sometimes as if trying to make up his mind about me. Friend or foe? Safe? But mostly he ignored me and it was better to let it be like that. He needed time. He was a very silent little boy, but would hold mumbled conversations with himself if he thought no one was listening. Rene tended to smother him with maternal enthusiasm, but Oliver had his measure better. They laughed together. Were easy.

He became a little easier with me as time went by. One day I was sitting on a rug on the lawn and he threw his ball rather close. I let it stay where it was and smiled at him. His face screwed up into annoyance so I pushed it towards him, but not near enough for him to reach. "Sometimes I feed the birds," I told him. "They come very close. They know I wouldn't hurt them."

Perhaps I shouldn't have used the word hurt. He knew it too well. His face was shadowed momentarily, became unchildlike. Oh, God, I thought, I'm sorry. Sorry! I turned my head away from him, biting my lip.

When I turned back he had crept nearer and was squatting down

53

holding the ball and looking at me. I tried to smile and then cupped my hands, "Throw. I'll catch."

He pondered this and then very hesitantly pushed the ball towards me. I pushed it back with equal care. Trust began to grow as we played.

I don't know how much contact he had with other children. He wasn't old enough for school and didn't attend play school. One Wednesday morning I searched through my book shelves and found some Beatrix Potter books I had kept since I was a child. My father had written on the flyleaf of one of them: 'To Maeve on her sixth birthday, from her loving Daddy.' My childhood had been cushioned with affection. I hadn't known what it was to be afraid.

That afternoon I gave the book to Wayne.

Rene told me I was being a fool. "He'll scribble on it. And it was from your Dad."

"It doesn't matter. I'd like him to have it."

We both watched as he took it to show Oliver. And then Oliver sat him on his knee and read the story to him. It was an acceptable gift from Oliver's point of view. An old tatty book that meant a lot to me.

Rene's values were different. She told me bluntly that same afternoon when we were fetching lemonade from the fridge that she and Oliver had had a bloody awful row over the clothes I'd bought for Wayne. She had wanted to keep them. Why not? "But, oh no, Maeve. Back they had to come. He has odd ideas. Had you been a social worker, or someone equally crappy, he would have taken them and not bothered."

She asked me what I'd done with them. I told her that I'd thought of giving them to one of the Barnardo shops but hadn't got around to it yet. "Shall I keep them and perhaps later on, when he's forgotten about them, I'll slip them back to you?"

She twisted her lips into a bitter little grin. "Nice idea, Flower, but I want to stay in one piece."

"Don't call me Flower." It was an irritating habit she'd picked up when we were inside. But I said it automatically, my mind busy trying to see another aspect of Oliver. He had pride. Okay. Understandable. They'd had an argument. Well, yes. But staying in one piece?

"He's surely never hit you?"

"Did I ever say he had?" She poured lemonade in the small beaker for Wayne and then stood looking around the kitchen. "Do you know – I'd like to make a cake, or a pudding or something. Is there time?"

They were always off the premises by five. An unspoken rule. Made by them. Not by me. But I was glad of it. They had sussed the situation. Correctly.

I said: "Yes – but you surely don't want . . . I mean, who eats cakes?" She was changing the subject, of course.

"Well, Christopher might," Rene suggested, trespassing in turn on my forbidden land. "The man you never talk about," she added.

"If you're serious about the cake," I said, "then – yes – there's time."

"Subject of Christopher closed," Rene said lightly.

I didn't answer.

The possibility that Christopher might return early one Wednesday was always at the back of my mind, but it never occurred to me that my mother might walk in on us. We were at the bottom of the garden eating a very early picnic tea. It was about three-thirty and Rene had spent the last hour making scones and ginger biscuits. The lawn had been neatly cut and edged and the mower put away. We were sitting around the white cane garden trolley and Wayne had his own little stool just beside it where he could kneel up and reach his plate. It was he who heard the car turning up the drive. He listened, his head a little on one side, and then suddenly got up and ran into the hydrangea bushes. Apart from his fright, there was some humour in the situation, I suppose. We didn't know what had startled him until my mother appeared around the side of the house and stood looking at us, equally startled.

"Darling," she said, coming over to me. "When I saw the van I thought you had workmen. I didn't know you had visitors."

My mother always dresses well. She looked impeccable in a linen suit in a soft shade of blue and her hair had been recently rinsed a pale silver. Both Rene and I were in jeans and cotton sweatshirts — mine yellow — hers a shade darker red than her hair. Oliver's working gear is a navy tracksuit worn with heavy shoes when he's mowing. He'd kicked them off and his naked feet, sun-tanned, slender, were difficult to ignore. Difficult for me. Difficult, for a different reason, for my mother.

She kissed me.

There was something terribly bothersome on her mind. All the signals were flashing at high speed. But courtesies had to be observed and she duly observed them. So did I.

I introduced her to my friends.

Rene, easy with everyone, was easy with her, too. "Hello," she said. "It's nice to meet Maeve's mum."

Oliver pushed his shoes back on, apologising. "It's so hot." He stood up and offered his deckchair. "Or would you prefer a high one? The lounger in the shed is more comfortable." He asked me if he should fetch it. I said yes, please.

The scenario was established.

I tried to see it through my mother's eyes. A man who knew where things were kept and liked to sit around with bare feet. A bosomy, pretty young woman, who obviously knew me very well.

And a little red-haired boy who was hiding in the bushes.

My mother noticed him. Smiled at him vaguely. Looked enquiringly at me. "He's shy," I said. "He'll come out in a minute."

"But don't pounce on him when he does," Rene warned. "He doesn't like being hugged."

My mother is not a hugger. It should have been evident.

She accepted the chair Oliver brought her, but declined Rene's biscuits and my offer of tea.

There was something she wanted to say to me — in private. I sensed this strongly and wondered what it was. We spoke about the garden for a while, though she didn't guess that Oliver had had a hand in it. He didn't deliberately hide the fact, it just didn't come up. She didn't ask him outright what he did. That would have been impolite. And when she put out feelers he ignored them.

Eventually she asked the question I was hoping she wouldn't.

She addressed it to Rene. "It's strange I haven't met you before. I thought I knew most of Maeve's friends. Where did you meet?"

Rene helped herself to a biscuit. Looked at me. Took a bite of the biscuit. Swallowed it. Looked at me again.

"Well," she said slowly, "this could be embarrassing."

"Not at all," I said brusquely. "Why should it be? Rene and I met in prison."

My mother flushed, the skin around her neck mottling. She pursed her lips. Gazed at Rene. Said nothing. The silence had the quality of brittle glass. I felt I wanted to punch it. Splinter it. I had forgotten how my mother could exude displeasure – no, that's too weak a word – contempt. Her attitude to me when I had been sentenced had been a mixture of grief, anger and shame. She had coped with it by seeing me as rarely as possible. Her letters had ignored the issue totally and been stilted recordings of social events. Addressing the envelopes to the prison must have given her pain. I had imagined her furtively posting them. Now, looking at Rene, she could have been examining a creature from a murky sub-culture.

I lied with absolutely no flicker of conscience whatsoever – impulsively – protectively. "Rene," I said, "is a prison visitor."

"*Was*," Oliver interposed, his dark eyes gleaming with amusement.

It took Rene a moment or two to pick it up. She could have joked about it, denied it, but guessing how I felt for her she didn't. She spoke with complete sincerity. "Maeve should never have been there. She keeps on saying I helped her. I don't know. We had a few chats about this and that. I know she expected you to visit more often and was hurt when you didn't."

The situation for my mother had boomeranged. She felt it was necessary to defend herself and didn't know what to say. "It's just that I . . . when you have a daughter you love . . . and she . . . in a place like that . . . I mean . . ." It was incoherent and she stopped trying.

"Prison is harder for some to take than others," Rene went on, quite gently, "but she took it as best she could – and now it's over – so there's not much point in talking about it any more." She glanced over at Wayne who was fiddling with his shorts. "Hang on, lovey, don't pee in your pants." She darted over to him and took him deeper behind the bush.

How my mother could believe in a prison visitor who came visiting with her family when the prisoner had been released was hard to understand. But she did believe. When Rene returned after seeing to Wayne her attitude towards her had changed. It was cool, but not frigid. "How old is your little boy?"

"Four."

"He has your colouring, but not your curls. Do you think he might be tempted out in a minute to talk to me?"

Rene explained that he spoke very little. "It's not that he's deaf – or daft – nothing like that."

"Oh, well," my mother said, tiring of the subject, "I'm sure when he starts chattering you won't be able to stop him." She turned to me. "Maeve, I wasn't going to say this in front of your friends – but obviously your friends know. My dear girl, what on earth possessed you to make the broadcast?"

"So you've seen the *Radio Times*? The interview isn't scheduled until next week. I was going to tell you." (Was I? Perhaps.)

The write-up had taken half a page and they'd used my passport photograph. A letter had come from Macbarra, quite a friendly one, with a scrawled p.s. in ink wishing me well.

"But for heaven's sake – why?"

"It was something I felt I had to do."

"You mean you were coerced?" She shook her head. "I can't believe it. You had freedom of choice. You should never have been persuaded." She went on like this for a while and finally turned to Oliver and Rene for support. "Given the circumstances, would you agree to making public exhibitions of yourselves?"

Unclear as to what she was talking about they made noncommittal noises.

I drew the picture for them.

They agreed I was crazy but said they'd listen in.

"Unfortunately," my mother said, "I won't be able to – though perhaps it's just as well. I'll be out of the country when it's transmitted."

She explained that she'd had a last minute invitation to go on a three months' cruise with a friend. "Her sister has had to back out due to illness, so I'm having her ticket."

I was delighted for her. "That's lovely. I'm so pleased. You haven't had a proper holiday for too long." I kissed her affectionately. "The last couple of years have been awful for you."

Her eyes filled with tears and I felt pangs of guilt. We mock. We hurt. But there's love there, too.

She went into details about the cruise, mainly to establish a safe level of coolness between us again. Emotion is treacherous. Tears are weak.

"While I'm away," she said, "my neighbours will look after the house, but the caravan at Shuters Cove is too far off the beaten track. I'll leave the keys with you and Christopher. Use it whenever you want to, and then see it's properly secured for the winter."

She stood up.

So did I.

We looked at each other for a long moment. "Everything," I said, "will be all right."

A vague promise. A pledge to the gods. An ordinary hope for good things to come. For all of us. I slipped my arm through hers and walked with her to her car.

It was after my mother had gone and I was sitting again with Rene and Oliver that the butterfly attacked Wayne. Or so it must have seemed to him. The gentle, fluttery little creature, bright yellow in the sunlight, was dancing around his head and, pale with terror, he was backing away from it. And then he began to moan, as if it were burning him, lacerating him. Oliver reached him just before Rene. He clapped the delicate thing between his hands, crushing it. Powdery, no longer beautiful, it drifted on to the lawn and he ground it into the grass with his heel. Wayne went down on his knees and curled himself up like an embryo. Rene squatted beside him and ran her fingers gently through his hair.

This was no ordinary phobia. Disturbed, not only by his reaction, but by his parents', too, I sat watching them. Oliver's expression warned me to do nothing, say nothing. They stayed quietly by the little boy, waiting for him to stand up again, to become calm. The uneasy silence seemed to last a long time.

As they were leaving, Rene referred to it when Wayne was out of earshot. "Kids," she said, "get bothered by different things. If it happens again – and we're not around – do what we did. He needs a bit of help . . . okay?" Her eyes were dark with worry, but she kept her tone of voice flippant. "With me," she said, "it's spiders."

6

On the day of the broadcast a drug addict ran amok with a gun and killed five people.

The news, which preceded the transmission by a couple of hours, was used by Christopher as a kind of anodyne. What I had done, he implied, was relatively minor. A mere peccadillo of a crime. "So calm your conscience, Maeve. Stop being so troubled. Try to be more at peace with yourself."

Last night I had the nightmare again and had turned to him shivering and he had held me while I told him about it. He can be tender, but he can't get inside my head and under my skin and stop me feeling. There is an undertone of impatience when he speaks to me.

Now, as we sit listening to the broadcast, he is rigid with embarrassment. It is a little after eight o'clock and the evening sun is streaming into the room, making it golden. There is whisky and water on the table beside him but he has only taken a few sips of it. I am well down my glass of gin and tonic. I had keyed myself up for this, but it's hard to believe that the voice I'm hearing is mine. The one phrase that rings true is the one about giving ten years of my life for the injury to Sergeant Sutherland not to have happened. Macbarra goes on to talk about my eighteen months inside prison. The broadcast has become a kind of patchwork of opinions – perhaps in order to fill out too short a programme. The prison governor describes me as "a very assured young woman with a very large chip on her shoulder." (Assured? How little you knew me. Chip? Is that how it seemed?)

My coping with the alien atmosphere by "closing off part of my mind – accepting what had to be accepted" is used as a platform for the psychiatrist to sound off. He admits we hadn't met – there were others in greater need – and then proceeds to generalise. It sounds like the usual textbook jargon. My lie about adjusting seems to make everyone happy, especially the chaplain who has a few words to say about Christian guidance, misplaced idealism in the nuclear context, and the thorny path to salvation. I remember his sermon about the pricks and begin to giggle almost hysterically.

Christopher half rises from his chair. "Let's turn the bloody thing off."

"No. I'm all right. It's just that it's so false. Not me. Nothing to do with me."

The last question and answer about corruption have been heavily edited, as I expected.

My voice – yes, *my* voice – prissy, far back – declaims about pain and frustration being everywhere. "There is no special breeding ground for corruption. Prison will corrupt some."

And there it stops abruptly.

My contribution ended, the experts continue the thesis.

They are so sure, the experts, so clinical. We, the other breed, are to be observed like creatures in a laboratory. A little of this therapy. A little of that. The criminal mind is laid bare on the dissecting table of their prejudices. But they are careful not to call it that. The word 'disturbed' is used euphemistically. Are they, themselves, so immune, so carefully placed inside their own fortresses of respectability that they are never 'disturbed'?

Why didn't Macbarra get some of the women officers to come and talk? The ones who saw the action and for the most part did the best they could. Too many cons. Tension on a high note. Therapy?

Macbarra finishes the talk with a few kind words about me. "A sensitive woman, deeply sorry for the injury she has caused. If she is listening to this broadcast then I wish her well."

Thank you, Macbarra. But don't be kind to me. Not just now. I can't stand it.

Christopher switches off the radio. "Pompous ass! He should never have talked you into it." He looks closely at me and I turn my head away. My eyes are burning and my throat feels as if it has been rasped raw.

"Well, it's over," Christopher says. "It shouldn't have happened, but it's over."

His disapproval stiffens me. I no longer feel the need to reach out to him as I did last night. He comforted my nightmare. I can't dispel his embarrassment.

The broadcast had repercussions we didn't expect. Friends re-emerged. I was apparently forgiven for spilling wine on Louella. We were back on the social scene. Invitations arrived for a dinner – a barbecue – a visit to the opera. I made polite excuses, but for Christopher's sake tried not to offend.

I couldn't understand people's attitudes. I still can't. What is so cleansing about a broadcast? Had I been washed whiter than white by the BBC?

I only feel completely at ease with Rene and Oliver. It occurs to me that I am now on their side of the divide. Seeing them every Wednesday, and getting closer to Wayne, does my heart good. I am being appallingly deceitful to Christopher, but I can't care.

The fact that Christopher might be deceiving me was brought to my notice by Samantha. She called round one morning after I'd refused a luncheon invitation on the pretext of having flu.

After the usual greeting, a touching of cheeks, she brushed past me into the sitting room then turned and observed me with a mixture of disapproval and amusement. "You don't look sick to me," she said brusquely.

I resisted smoothing my hair, which was a mess, and stuck my hands in my pockets. I looked a slouch but, no, I didn't look sick.

She looked marvellous. A dark-eyed thirty-six-year-old woman who knew how to present herself. A flattering Cleopatra-style fringe accentuated her high cheekbones. Her cream suede suit, expertly tailored, disguised her too-large hips. I told her I liked her new hairdo. But as a diversionary tactic it didn't work.

She gestured impatiently and a couple of tortoiseshell bracelets jangled together like muted drums. "Never mind me. I'm here to talk about you. For goodness sake, Maeve, I know that dinner party you came to some while ago was pretty disastrous, but everyone's nerves were strung. It would be different now. You've got over it."

"Good," I said. "Nice to know. What will you have? Coffee? Whisky? Gin?"

"Coffee." She came to the kitchen while I made it and helped to set out the cups on a tray. Her fingernails were a bronze pink. She glanced around the room. "Don't you have a cleaning woman any more?"

I wondered if she was referring to the blobs of grease on the cooker. "No. I manage."

"I know of an au-pair. She's better than most."

"No thanks."

She glanced at my unvarnished nails but didn't comment.

I poured the coffee and we took it through to the sitting room. She took a chair by the window in the full sun. "Your garden's looking all right. You share your man with Louise, don't you?"

For a moment I thought of Oliver. I only wished he were mine to share. Loyalty to Rene put the brakes on. You might fancy your best friend's husband, but unless you're the lowest form of life you don't entice him.

"I was under the impression," Samantha went on, "that Louise had lost him – sick or something. I think she called him Williams – or Walker? Perhaps I've got it wrong."

"Perhaps," I agreed.

"So he's still coming to you?"

"As you see – my lawns are still being cut."

"Okay," she smiled, "be cagey. If you're paying him more than Louise is, then you're entitled to grab him for an extra day."

She changed the subject and said what she had come to say. "I've just heard about Christopher's new assistant. According to Paul, she was taken on a couple of months ago. Same qualifications as you – a degree in accountancy. I thought you would have been offered the job."

I tried not to show surprise, but didn't succeed. Samantha is hawk-eyed. Christopher had spoken about the work load being heavy for his partner and himself. There was efficient secretarial back-up, of course. He might have said something about employing a qualified assistant. If he had I couldn't remember.

"Husbands and wives don't work too well together," I hedged.

Samantha wasn't deceived. I hadn't known. She proceeded to enlighten me. "She's the daughter of one of Paul's friends in Chambers. Harrington, the QC. Her name is Sarah and she's about twenty-four. Small – not much of a dresser – but, for all that, according to Paul, quite a dish."

She sipped her coffee. "Do you want to hear the rest of it?"

If she expected my stomach to clench in horrified anticipation she was disappointed. "If there's more to hear, you'll tell me anyway."

She shrugged. "Darling, we've been friends a long time. And I don't want to sound alarm bells. Nothing is clanging too loudly at the moment. Just lunch most days in that Spanish restaurant down the road from Christopher's office. Probably an ordinary working relationship. A handy place to eat."

"Probably."

"Men need companionship," she went on. "It can be risky if they're denied it. Not as bad as denying them sex, but almost as dangerous." She considered this. "Perhaps more dangerous. Casual sex isn't hard to come by. Companionship can lead to a lasting relationship." She leaned forward, smiling, her head on one side. "Now take a swipe at me if you think I'm being impertinent."

I assured her that these days I was well controlled.

"Get even better controlled," she advised. "Start accepting invitations. Take a good long hard look at Christopher. He's an attractive man."

Samantha is a gossip, but in this instance I believe she meant well. And what she said was sensible. Christopher and I are in many ways ill-matched. There was strong sexual attraction when we married, and that was more important than our differences.

Nowadays we make love rather like two strangers on a desert island with just the bond of propinquity. No, perhaps that's not fair. I don't know what he feels. How can I?

But I know what I don't feel.

I feel no shock – no anger – no jealousy. As yet there's no reason to. If Samantha had given me news of Christopher bedding – what's her name? – Sarah – every lunch time, then perhaps I might have been emotionally stung. As it was, my reaction was almost indifferent – almost, not quite.

He has always cared for me. Disapproved. Been annoyed. But never deliberately hurt me. I have been totally self-centred. Infuriating. And not much good in any practical way.

I should try considering him more. Go to places with him, if that's what he wants. He has been as tolerant as his nature allows.

If Christopher noticed a change in my attitude he didn't comment on it. I suggested that we should spend a week-end at my mother's caravan and he agreed without any show of reluctance. He knew I was fond of the place, that it had associations with my father. It's in a field, a couple of minutes' walk from a sheltered cove, and has wonderful views of the sea. It's glorious when the sun shines and rather bleak when it doesn't. It didn't shine for us. Chilly, and with not much to talk about, we wandered along the beach and climbed the cliff path. I didn't ask him about his new assistant and he didn't mention her. We spent two uncomfortable nights on the bunk beds, ate unappetising food cooked on a paraffin stove, mainly fried bacon and stews that could be boiled in tins, and drove home with relief.

It wasn't very successful, but I had tried.

The next suggestion came from him. A few days together in Paris.

"Why?" I asked him.

"Why not?" he countered.

Because I won't be home on Wednesday, I thought.

"No reason," I said, "if that's what you want."

"I want you to be happy. We could have a good time together." He added, rather awkwardly, "Again."

I ached with momentary love for him – a flash of guilt and pain – a swift memory of how it had once been between us.

"All right," I agreed, "let's go."

Paris gave us sunshine, culture, and *haute cuisine*. Christopher zealously tracked down gourmet restaurants, including Maxim's, and an excellent little place in the Latin Quarter where the wine waiter looked like Oliver. He also tracked down the Eglise du Dôme and stood in awe before Napoleon's tomb while I stood patiently beside him. Reluctantly he gave the Musée de l'Armée a miss and came to the Louvre with me instead. We were being oh so tactful, both of us. On our last night we went to a performance of Bellini's *La Sonnambula* at the Opéra, then strolled back to the hotel along the rue de la Paix, passing Cartier which was closed. He suggested we should return there in the morning before catching our plane home and buy some little memento. As a little memento from Cartier was a contradiction in terms – and surely he couldn't be that rich or that guilty about Sarah – I declined. He'd already bought me a pair of shoes, I pointed out, and they'd cost the earth. I didn't want anything else.

Back at the hotel, after drinking the contents of a couple of miniature bottles of Scotch from the drinks cabinet in the bedroom, we made love. Gently, briefly, and without excitement. As always Christopher slept almost immediately, but sleep came uneasily to me as if I were slowly moving downwards into something dark and frightening. The full impact of the nightmare about Sutherland struck in the small hours.

It was as bad as it had ever been. I could smell the mud. Feel the skin of his face. When I was able to move I went into the adjoining bathroom and sat on the side of the bath, trembling. Reorientation took a long time. I touched the marbled wall tiles, shook heavily perfumed talc on my feet, buried my face in the stiff folds of the shower curtains, told myself that this was the Ritz Hotel in the Place Vendôme not a field in Langdon. Gradually I came to believe it. When I returned to the bedroom Christopher was mumbling in his sleep. I wished he would awaken and comfort me, but he turned on his side and slept on. I got in beside him, but didn't dare sleep again. In the morning he told me anxiously that I looked tired. I didn't tell him why.

The flight back to Heathrow was bumpy and the traffic heavy as we drove home. It was late afternoon when we turned into the driveway and we were both glad to get out of the car. Christopher went round to the boot to fetch the luggage while I found the house keys and opened the front door. As I stepped across the threshhold, the thin heels of my new shoes pressed into something soft and lumpy – a manilla envelope lying face down on the mat. I picked it up and turned it over. MAEVE was printed across it in violet ink. Puzzled, I ripped it open. Inside was a dirty white rag with the CND logo carefully drawn on it with a rusty-looking substance. It took me a moment or two to realise it was blood.

7

I had never before felt menaced. This was in a different league from the sick mail I'd received after being released from prison. The threat was implicit in the blood – no words needed. And it had been put through the letter-box. Not posted. Someone had prowled around the property while we were away.

I sat on the stairs, too weak with shock to move from where I had picked it up. There were other letters on the floor – a seed catalogue – the telephone bill – a post-card, probably from my mother. The afternoon seemed so bright and normal. Sun on a silver rose bowl on the hall table. The grandfather clock ticking quietly. We had been home less than five minutes.

Christopher, about to carry the suitcase upstairs, looked at me, puzzled. "Why are you sitting there? What's the matter?"

I handed him the envelope and the bloodied scrap of rag.

He was livid with rage. "This is a matter for the police."

"No."

"What do you mean – no? I can't handle this for you. The police will have to be brought in."

"And what do you expect them to do – other than gloat?"

"Gloat? Jesus Christ, Maeve! What are you talking about?"

I couldn't control the words that came tumbling out. "I hurt one of them – and then I get this – a reminder of blood spilt – what do you expect them to do – say sorry, Mrs. Barclay – a very unpleasant experience, Mrs. Barclay – or goddamnit woman, you deserved it?"

"You're hysterical. You don't know what you're saying."

"Oh yes, I do. I know them. The fuzz. It's them and us. You're all right. You're one of them. On their side. I've been behind bars – remember?"

"Do you suppose you'll ever let me forget?" It was deeply bitter.

We cooled down eventually, became calm. He helped me off with my anorak and took me through to the living room. I don't like brandy but he made me take a few sips.

He began talking about having the blood tested forensically. "It could lead to whoever sent this."

Of the two I was the more rational now. "If I were lying dead – murdered – then it would be tested. Under these circumstances the fuzz wouldn't bother. There are a few million people out there – some of them crazy – with that sort of blood. The best thing we can do with it is burn it."

Fire is clean. I wanted to see the revolting thing curling up into blackness. It took some while before he agreed. And then he let me do it, snatching the lighter from my hands just before I burnt my fingers.

From that time on he began to be nervous about my safety. I was not to open the door to strangers. A peep-hole was inserted, also a chain. He suggested I might like a dog. I told him I wouldn't. If I had an animal at all I'd have a cat . . . a Persian, perhaps. He told me I was being facetious, that my moods were impossible, and to stop calling the police 'fuzz'. His reference to the police was pulled out of the air as another topic for dissent. I hadn't recently mentioned them.

For a while I became the stronger one, calming him.

It was Oliver who tried to calm me.

For the last few Wednesdays the garden had been untended. Wayne, according to a phone call from Oliver, had chicken-pox.

I offered to visit, but he said no, better not. They'd all be along together, soon. Rene sent her love. Okay?

Okay. But I missed them.

Last Wednesday he came on his own. Wayne was better, he said, but hadn't started going out yet. Next week perhaps. He didn't know.

He did his usual gardening chores. The weather wasn't good, but the rain didn't seem to bother him. I fussed about his getting wet and made him a bowl of hot soup. He sat across the kitchen table from me, smelling of damp tracksuit, and we tried to make conversation without much success. He sensed my tension and wanted to know what was bothering me.

I told him about the grotesque contents of the envelope – my guilt about Sergeant Sutherland – the nightmares. He had a knack of listening and saying very little, but what he did say showed warmth and understanding. He dismissed the bloodied rag as a piece of rubbish done on impulse by a screwed-up creep, and advised me to forget it. He took the rest of it more seriously.

"Being in stir is like being ill – for people like you. And I mean *you*. There are plenty of classy bitches in there who don't give a shit. You'll get over it one day. But you may need to see Sergeant Sutherland first."

This seemed so unlikely that I hadn't an answer.

We were usually careful not to touch each other, but as I sat there thinking over what he had told me, he pushed the empty soup bowl aside, got up, and walked round to my side of the table. He put his hands on my shoulders and gently massaged my neck muscles.

"It relaxes Rene," he said.

Maybe so. It wasn't relaxing me. It was electrifying me. I wanted him to hold me. Take me upstairs. Make love to me. We were alone together in the house. The opportunity, the need, was there.

I pulled away from him.

I couldn't see his eyes, but I heard him sigh softly. His voice was rueful. "Rene likes it."

"Rene's the lucky one."

My meaning must have been very clear. Loyalty with a capital L.

He returned to his side of the table. "So's your husband," he said drily.

Before he left I took him through to the study where most of the books are kept and gave him another book for Wayne. "It's *The Tailor of Gloucester*. One of my favourites when I was his age. Read it to him before he goes to sleep."

Wayne. A safe topic.

He barely glanced at it, but looked around the room, aware perhaps that this was Christopher's very personal territory. There was a monogrammed cigarette lighter on the desk next to a small photograph of me taken on our honeymoon. On the back of the chair by the desk Christopher's grey pullover hung untidily, its sleeves dangling.

"Wayne will like the story," I assured him. "Most kids do."

He tried to show interest in the book, turning over the pages. "He liked the other. Keeps it by his bed."

"Good."

"He's getting easy with you. Talks about you. He was upset he couldn't come today. He's very cooped up in the flat. There's nowhere for him to play."

I knew that. It was a dreary hole.

It was on impulse that I suggested that he might like to have the use of the caravan for a week-end now and then. "It's a good place for a family holiday. Good for Wayne to have some sea air."

I went to fetch the keys and a map of the district.

When I returned he was sitting at the desk and Christopher's pullover had fallen on the floor. He got up, looking embarrassed, and retrieved it. "Sorry!"

"Sorry for what? Don't be ridiculous." I tried to persuade him to sit again, but he wouldn't.

Standing together we studied the map and I drew the route in pencil. "A small caravan," I said. "Just room enough for the three of you."

"Then you won't come, too?"

The dark quizzical eyes probed the extent of my commitment.

I told him I wouldn't. "But phone me before you go.

Christopher and I have recently been, but he might decide to go again – and so . . ."

If Oliver thought there were degrees of loyalty – sexual and all the other kinds – he didn't comment.

I walked out with him to his motorbike. The rain had eased off and the air smelt of warm soil and flowers.

"I might be able to put you in touch with Sergeant Sutherland," he offered, just before leaving. "If that's what you want."

I was so surprised I didn't know what to say.

"If that's what you want," he repeated.

"But how can you? I don't understand. How can you possibly – I mean what sort of authority have you? You don't know him – or do you . . .?"

He agreed he didn't know him. But he knew others who did. The others, I guessed, didn't wear neat uniforms and drive panda cars.

But Sutherland himself was legit.

And it might be good for me to speak to him.

I was so bothered I began to sweat with indecision.

"I don't know. I just don't know."

"Well, think about it," Oliver said calmly. "No hurry to decide."

A shared double bed is not the best place to worry in. That Christopher was also lying sleepless, though pretending to be relaxed, was obvious to me. He was still concerned about security. Some houses in the road had been burgled. Ours, despite our ropy alarm system, was so far untouched. The possibility of a break-in didn't bother me as much as having to make my mind up about Sergeant Sutherland. And about Oliver. Until now I had seen him as Rene's husband – Wayne's father – firmly fixed in a domestic environment. When he roamed free, where did he roam? And with whom?

Christopher spoke to me in the darkness. "Are you awake, Maeve?"

"Yes."

"Is anything the matter?"

"No."

73

He sat up and put the bedside light on. "I had a talk with Colonel Claythorpe today. He and some of our other neighbours are starting a Neighbourhood Watch. I agreed to take part. I said you would, too."

"Shouldn't you have asked me first?"

"It's to your benefit. I naturally didn't tell him about that appalling piece of rag. But I haven't been easy about you since it was pushed through the letter-box. If he, or any of the others, see strangers around the place, they'll tell us. Alert the police if necessary."

Oh, God! I thought. Oliver's van — old, battered, grotty — arriving every Wednesday would send the whole toffee-nosed, Mercedes-driving bunch into a frenzy of speculation.

It was obviously time to tell Christopher I had changed my gardener. But how? He'd probe. Ask how I'd heard about him, what testimonials he'd got. My imagination and my tongue seized up in a kind of moral paralysis. I muttered something about needing to go to the lavatory.

When I returned Christopher was lying down again, his hands cupped behind his head. He had his ready-to-make-love expression, but when I got in beside him he made no move to touch me.

My confession, about to be thrust reluctantly into words, was abruptly pushed back by his.

"We had a vacancy in the office a while back. I didn't think you were ready for work. If I had I would have told you. I think I might have been wrong. Getting out every day would be better than hanging around here."

I said something vague about Samantha mentioning someone called Sarah.

"Eric's choice," he said. "She's competent. I'm sorry you had to hear it from Samantha. What the hell has it to do with her, anyway?"

"Nothing," I soothed. "You and Eric choose your own staff."

And I choose my own gardener — so let it be. At least temporarily.

Christopher put his hand on my breast and fingered it gently. "Eric's wife, Sue, is in hospital — complications with a pregnancy. High blood pressure, or something."

A hint that we should try for a child?

"He's eating out quite a bit. Would you mind having him round for dinner one night this week?"

Not a hint. Nothing to do with a child. "Just Eric?"

He stopped feeling my nipple and returned his hand to his side. "Perhaps Sarah as well. She's met Sue socially. And she knows most of our crowd. Except you. What do you say?"

"If that's what you want."

"I'm quite indifferent. It just seems a friendly gesture, that's all."

His indifference doesn't sound like indifference to me, but I'm not in any position to question it. "Why not? A friendly gesture would be very nice. Let's make it this Friday, shall we?" I nearly ask him if Sarah likes Spanish food, but stop myself in time.

He reaches up and puts the light out. Bothered, I think, by my tone of voice. "Well – that's it, then. Friday, if it suits everyone. Your first dinner party since . . ." He lets it trail.

"Yes." I don't finish the sentence for him. Prison has become a forbidden word. I have used it too often.

I spent Thursday cleaning the kitchen for Sarah. It was a tip. She might pity Christopher for being lumbered with me, but she couldn't pity him because the cooker didn't shine. And the food had better be good. While I scrubbed away I worked out a menu in my head. Avocado for a starter. Easy. A duck with trimmings. Not too difficult. Profiteroles – or meringues – or something – to follow. Not brilliant, but the best I could manage.

Men, as a rule, don't bring their lovers home. Or do they? As a catalyst for improving the environment Sarah has been effective. I'm curious about her, but feel nothing deeper. I suppose in this sort of situation a wife would buy a new dress. I have many dresses and feel no urge to compete. The green silk will do, worn with the aquamarine pendant Christopher bought me when we were in Greece. He has always been generous. In every way.

It is so easy to tot up his virtues, and be unmoved by them. That he should stray is natural. That I should be so uncaring is not.

How would Rene react if Oliver and I . . .?

As I would, if Oliver belonged to me and she trespassed.

I blank out the thought. Afraid of it.

Oliver arrived on his motorbike at four o'clock on Friday afternoon – three hours before the dinner party.

The kitchen smelt of oranges soaking in brandy and the duck, uncooked and about to be stuffed, was on the table. He came around to the back door, taking a chance that Christopher wouldn't be there.

"If you want to see Sergeant Sutherland," he said, without preamble, "and don't mind riding pillion on the bike, I can take you to him now."

My hands began shaking and I dropped a small blue bowl I was holding. It shattered. I let the pieces lie. "You mean – take me to his home?"

"No. A small park north of the river. A bloke I know has arranged to meet him there. You can speak to him – or not – as you choose."

He adds: "I have a spare helmet. You'll need to change into jeans and a warm jacket. If you're coming."

I gesture vaguely. "A dinner party."

He glances around the kitchen. Impatient. Obviously on edge. "Then you're not . . ."

For Christ's sake, I think, there are priorities. Surely Sergeant Sutherland tops the list.

He tore up that letter you sent him. And rightly. Do you suppose he'll feel any differently about you now?

This is a chance to know. To make an act of contrition. To purge my mind of memories. To see him as he is now.

I ask Oliver how long it will take to get there and back. ("How many miles to Babylon? Three score and ten. Will I get there by candle-light? Yes and back again.") The rhyme floats in and out of my mind as if I'm going crazy with nerves. I feel sick.

"The bloke he's meeting is due at five. I can get you there just before. If we move now. Pretty fast. Are you coming?"

"Yes."

Wearing a heavy helmet and clutching Oliver around the waist as we roared off on his machine my mind became mercifully blank. Survival was imperative. Traffic was heavy, but the bike weaved in and out expertly and he knew the side roads. The skin of my face was cold and my legs shaky when we arrived. With the engine shut off there was a remarkable feeling of peace and I sat a moment before he helped me off.

"Your hands are cold. I should have reminded you to wear gloves." He held his out to me. "Put these on, they'll warm you."

They were only a little too big, warm with his warmth.

I wanted to keep standing there, making no decision. The park, a small one, had at one time been a private garden for the surrounding houses. It was at most an acre. Purple and white hebe bushes grew thickly under chestnut trees. I saw a squirrel flashing like a rat across one of the concrete paths. Its movement broke the stillness and made my mind come alive again.

I had a clear vision of the field outside Langdon. The peaceful demonstrators, arms linked, a human barrier across the gates. Quiet singing of a hymn tune. The sudden unexpected eruption of violence. My violence. Forcing my way through the crowds to get to Sutherland. Kneeling by him. The taste of my blood as I bit my lip in horror. His blood darkly oozing down his cheek.

"You don't have to speak to him," Oliver said. "But if you want to, there's no time to hang around."

I gave him his gloves back. "Where can I find him?"

He walked over to the entrance with me. "Go down the main path until you get to the wooden arch with a bushy plant climbing over it. Turn left and you'll see some steps leading up to a fancy-looking wall. There's a seat quite close. He should be there."

"And if he's not?"

He was obviously holding on to his patience. "Then I've got it wrong, haven't I?"

"The man he's arranged to meet . . ."

"What about him?"

"Does he know about me?"

"Why the f . . ." he broke off. "No, he doesn't. Why should he? This is your scene, Maeve. Go play it if you want to."

I hesitated. It would be easy to get back on the machine and get him to take me home. Now.

77

"Whatever you decide," he said, "I'll meet you here later. Now move."

Inside the park amongst the trees it was claustrophobic. The place was overgrown. Untended. The wooden arch was a rotting pergola held together with honeysuckle. Smells, sweet and earthy, cloyed. I walked on, obeying Oliver's command and ignoring my instinct to turn back.

There was no one sitting on the bench.

I strolled past it, relieved.

He came as a distant clock struck five. A neat-looking man wearing tweeds and with a Cairn terrier trotting beside him. In my worst moments I had imagined a guide dog and a white stick. In my nightmares he had been hideously scarred. Now, all I could see was a cicatrix on his cheekbone – a puckered area of flesh. His eyes, behind tinted glasses, looked normal, and he walked with confidence.

I recognised him in the moment he recognised me.

Mutually embarrassed we turned from each other.

I walked down the path as far as the balustrade and stood leaning against it and gazed down at the garden below, my heart thudding and my breathing harsh and laboured. I took some deep gulps of air then breathed in and out slowly, gradually becoming calmer.

The dog came and sniffed at my heels. If Sergeant Sutherland was on an assignment why had he brought his dog? Weren't pubs the more usual places for the plain clothes fuzz to meet their contacts?

Fuzz. Don't use the word. Not about him. That's the man you hurt. Stop crouching behind your barrier of guilt. Turn round. Look at him. Go over to him.

I couldn't move.

It was Sergeant Sutherland who approached me. "Mrs. Barclay?"

My breathing was easier now and I was able to answer normally. "Yes."

"I imagine you must have some purpose in being here. What is it?"

I hadn't heard him speak before. His voice was light, quite

pleasant, but when I looked at him the animosity showed in his eyes. Naturally. I hadn't expected it to be different.

A scenario in which I lay prostrate with remorse at his feet had troubled me for a long time, but now it gradually faded. The injury I had caused him wasn't as terrible as I had imagined. The wound was barely visible. His impaired vision didn't seem to inhibit him. I felt guilty about feeling less guilty. I had paid for a couple of seconds of uncontrolled stupidity with eighteen months in gaol. Deservedly. I had suffered nightmares. Deservedly. But no longer in my dreams would his blood mingle with my tears. It was over. Oliver's cure had worked.

He was waiting for an answer.

I told him I was taking a walk.

He didn't believe me. "So far from home?"

So he knew where I lived.

I shrugged.

"I heard your broadcast – and your reference to me. If your being here now is anything to do with that, then forget it. As you see, I've recovered."

"Yes." I added: "I'm sorry it happened – deeply sorry – and glad you're better."

It sounded trite. It *was* trite. I hadn't meant it to sound that way, but couldn't express it any differently. The anti-climax of this contrived meeting in some way diminished me. I was ashamed.

He glanced at his watch. "It's ten past five. I was expecting someone. Not you." His eyes behind the tinted glasses narrowed with conjecture. "Who sent you here?"

"No one. Why should anyone send me here?"

Oliver hadn't forced me to come. Don't mention him. Be careful.

"I can't believe your being here is a coincidence. If it isn't, you're keeping very dubious company, Mrs. Barclay. It's one of the hazards of being inside."

He must be referring to Oliver and Rene. When do the fuzz lay off? Do they bug ex-prisoners' phones? Watch who comes and goes?

"I'm warning you for your own good." He spoke with slow emphasis. "Pick up your life and get on with it sensibly. Prison

79

isn't a disaster unless you make it so." He touched his cheek in what seemed to be an involuntary gesture. "I suppose, in a way, we've harmed each other. But you can't re-make the past. Don't ruin your future."

The dog had left us and was whining at a short, stocky man who was approaching from the far side of the pergola. Sutherland, dismissing me abruptly, went to meet him.

In retrospect I realise he was being kinder to me than I deserved, but what I saw as his criticism of Oliver and Rene seemed uncalled-for and it rankled. Go home, little girl. Choose your playmates with care.

When I reached the park gates Oliver wasn't waiting for me. Perhaps he had parked the motorbike somewhere else and had gone to fetch it. After half an hour I guessed he hadn't and didn't know what to do. I had no money on me so couldn't go home by bus. The only way back was by taxi, paying on arrival. But in this area taxis were few and far between and it took ages to flag one down.

I was anxious, not angry. He wouldn't have deliberately abandoned me. So where was he? What was wrong?

The worry of a ruined dinner party niggled, but placed in context wasn't important. I arrived home half an hour before the guests were due to arrive.

8

Christopher, fuming, demanded an explanation. I told him I'd explain later. Just now there wasn't time.

"Was this a calculated insult to Eric and Sarah?" he persisted, following me to the kitchen. "And what the hell did you intend doing about the bloody duck?"

"Nothing," I told him. It was too late to cook it.

He laid the table while I scrabbled through the packets of frozen food in the deep freeze and came up with a Chinese concoction with rice. To serve the orange sauce with it would be bizarre, but there were no rules against it. The avocado, harmless and as yet unadorned with prawns or anything else, was probably best kept that way. The pudding, fresh fruit salad and cream, was abandoned for tinned fruit salad and cream.

Perhaps they wouldn't have educated palates. I haven't. Anyway, food is only food.

Why didn't Oliver wait for me?

Christopher, very clipped, suggested I should take a bath. "Your jeans – for God's sake *jeans* – smell of petrol."

The bell rang.

He looked at me in disgust. "I'll see to them while you get cleaned. Make excuses for you."

"Thanks," I said drily. "You can say there's been a breakdown in communication."

"A mental breakdown," he retorted caustically, "might describe it better." I couldn't think of a reply.

Sarah is a very cool, very beautiful brunette. She is wearing a calf-length, tweedy-looking skirt and a simple, low-cut white blouse. Not a brilliant dresser, as Samantha said, but she doesn't need to be. Her one piece of jewellery is a gold chain.

I was in such a hurry to get into my green silk that I burst the zip, luckily near the top, and fastened it with a safety pin. A lurex waistcoat hid the pin. I felt like a Christmas tree, lit on every branch and giving off sparks. I needed peace and a darkened room.

I needed to know what had happened to Oliver.

Sarah and I greet each other. I have a feeling that she might have been rather apprehensive about meeting me, but now that she has seen me all fear has fled. I am a clown. An impulsive idiot of a woman who does terrible things at nuclear dumps. A wife who plays on her husband's nerves so that he spills the sherry. (Not a lot. Just a few drops on the salver.)

I apologise for being late.

Tell Sarah I am so glad we are able to meet at last.

Kiss Eric and ask for Sue.

Smile at Christopher.

There is a pecking order in every group. In this one Sarah leads the team. She doesn't speak very much and she doesn't appear dominant, but she has an aura of quiet command. Eric is almost obsequious with her. Tubby, sandy, unromantic, nice Eric. You're the senior partner in the firm, Eric, but she'll climb on your shoulders if you'll let her. And you'll let her.

And she'll climb into Christopher's bed. Has climbed. Probably.

I sip my drink and watch them covertly.

Christopher likes his women young. If he craves for stability – and obviously he must – he would have done better with someone older. Sarah will play with him for a little and then move on . . . up. He deserves better from both of us. At times such as now I feel protective towards him. I want to put my arms around him and snarl at anyone who might hurt him. Ours is a complex relationship. I don't understand it. Most of the time I think I feel nothing and then surprise myself with a rush of tenderness. If you're going to leave me, Christopher, choose your lover with care. The next time your marriage should be good.

Eric's marriage is happy and normal. Well, he makes it sound that way and it probably is. It's Eric's conversation that helps the meal along. He tells us about Sue and her pregnancy – and his two older children who are in boarding school. And then waffles on about the educational system. He is so hungry, poor man, that he eats everything with enthusiasm. Sarah, trying not to look surprised, pushes the food around her plate. She asks me if I have any plans to resume my career at any stage. Obviously she didn't know that I was a possible contender for the job Christopher gave her. I tell her I have no plans. "Sometimes I think it would be nice to have a child."

This is spoken impulsively and I'm immediately sorry I've said it. It sounds devious. A getting back at her and Christopher. Embarrassing both of them. I don't fight that way. Even so, I meant it. I'm fond of Oliver's child. Of Oliver's and *Rene*'s child.

I would like a child of my own.

It was getting on for ten o'clock and we were at the coffee and brandy stage when Colonel Claythorpe called. He is a thick-set, white-haired, very shy man, too sensitive, one would suspect, to survive the army life, let alone do well in it. He and I have seen little of each other, but what we've seen we've liked. Well, *I've* liked, and I sense he may disapprove of my politics but not of me. When he came into the living room he looked at me rather oddly. I couldn't fathom the look. It was as if he wanted to reach out and touch me. My being there somehow reassured him. That there were others there, too, caused him some embarrassment. Having come, I sensed, he wanted to go, but was steeling himself to stay. He apologised rather awkwardly for disrupting a social gathering, as he rather quaintly put it, but that he would appreciate having a few words with me in private. I had a strong feeling that this was to exclude Christopher.

Christopher guessed this, too, but would have none of it. He made only a half-hearted attempt to persuade Sarah and Eric to stay a while longer when they suggested tactfully that they should take their leave. Eric, his curiosity held well in check, said warmly that he'd enjoyed the evening. Sarah, her cheek pressed coolly against mine, said the same. We all agreed to meet again for a meal soon.

Back in the living room the colonel was standing stiffly by the fireplace. He refused Christopher's offer of a brandy. He even refused to be seated. "I just had to come," he said, "to make sure Mrs. Barclay was all right."

"All right?" Christopher's voice was sharp with astonishment. "Why shouldn't she be all right?"

Colonel Claythorpe explained that the police had been visiting his home a few times. "We've been burgled, as I think you know. They've been finger-printing. Getting details and so on. This evening Sergeant Lamont called again – a Sèvres vase had been found at an antique shop. It seemed similar to the one that had been stolen from me. We compared photographs. They weren't identical. And then he . . ." He paused, looked at me. "And then he wanted to know about you, Mrs. Barclay. Had I seen you leave home this afternoon on the back of a red Kawasaki motorcycle?"

Christopher drew his breath in sharply, and then began smiling with amused disbelief. I reached out for my glass of brandy. There was very little in it. I sipped, then added more. I wished my hand would stop trembling. There was a sharp pain of apprehension in my gut.

The colonel glanced at Christopher and then at me. Aware of my distress, his embarrassment was growing by the minute. "I was pruning the roses at the time, and I did see you. He wanted to know the time you left here and I couldn't tell him that accurately. Around four, I thought. Just before tea."

Christopher was no longer amused. "I don't understand any of this. Maeve has never been on a motorcycle in her life. You must have made a mistake." He frowned at me, irritated that I didn't come up with an explanation. A forceful denial.

I swirled the brandy around my glass. Watched the amber liquid. Said nothing.

"I know the police have a job to do," the colonel continued, "and as neighbours we have to care for each other. But without intruding. I wouldn't have come here this evening if I hadn't been so worried. It seemed odd that the police should take such interest. I resented it, at the time. I mean, the fact that you'd recently been released from . . . well, I think you know what I'm trying to say . . . you've served your . . . and you . . . well, now it's over . . . you deserve respect and privacy." He was floundering and gestured helplessly. "The sergeant wanted to know if I'd seen you return – and when I said no, and had there been an accident? – he said no, not as far as he knew . . . and then he refused to say any more. I had the uncomfortable feeling that you might have been tricked into going somewhere, and perhaps held against your will. A stupid idea, but the circumstances seemed so odd. And the sergeant's interest was undeniably quite strong . . . amounting, I thought, to concern."

He shrugged, grimaced, and then took a few steps over to the door. "Anyway, that's the way I saw it. Perhaps stupidly. I knew I couldn't rest tonight without knowing you were safely home. I'm so relieved you are, and most awfully sorry I've disrupted your evening, caused your guests to leave. Upset you."

I thanked him for his kindness in coming. "It's good of you. As you can see, all is well." It's amazing how calm we sound when we're not.

When Christopher returned to me after seeing the colonel to the door, I had refilled my brandy glass almost to the brim. Not that I intended drinking that much. My hand just wouldn't control the bottle. My fingers felt boneless.

Christopher took the glass from me. "You don't like the stuff. Don't start being dramatic. Just explain what happened."

When Christopher sounds reasonable in a crisis it means his mind is as sharp and clear as ice. He would have made a first-class barrister, certainly better than the one at my trial. I knew before I spoke that it would be impossible to present Oliver to him in any way that would be acceptable, but I had to try.

"The owner of the motorcycle is Oliver Dudgeon. This afternoon he took me to meet Sergeant Sutherland. In a park. I needed to meet him. I'd been having bad dreams about him. Well, you

85

know that. He looked a lot better than I expected. His face is only slightly scarred, and his sight doesn't seem to be badly impaired. He did me a favour by taking me to him. I had to make a quick decision about going. That's why I mucked up the dinner tonight. I'm sorry."

It had all come out in a low monotone, rather deadpan, as if I didn't care very much.

"Sutherland?" Obviously what I'd told Christopher was even more surprising than the motorcycle ride. "But he tore up your letter. Refused to have any contact with you."

"That was some while ago. He was willing to speak to me. I feel a lot happier now I've seen him. I was going to tell you all this anyway, after the others had gone."

The emphasis was on Sutherland. It was better that way. Christopher, after apparently mulling it over in his mind, changed the emphasis.

"This man – the motorcyclist – Dudgeon. Is he a friend of Sergeant Sutherland?"

"I don't know. Perhaps a friend of a friend."

He looked at me suspiciously, aware I was prevaricating.

"Maeve – who is Dudgeon?"

"The husband of one of my friends."

"Which one?"

"Rene."

He has a good memory. "That red-headed woman who left prison the same day as you? Her husband picked her up on a motorbike."

"Yes."

"Oh, Christ!" He lost his cool temporarily and thumped his fist into the palm of his hand. "You're trying to tell me that this Dudgeon – this member of the criminal fraternity – makes some sort of connection with a police officer on your behalf? I find that impossible to believe."

I replied hotly that I was perfectly sure that Oliver hadn't a criminal record – but I had and Rene had and we'd gone through all the degradations of prison together and emerged good friends. And I was damned if I'd ditch her – or Oliver.

He became cold and analytical again. "You're telling me that you've been seeing them, that you've kept up this friendship since you came out?"

"Yes."

"Where and how often?"

"I'm not a prisoner in the dock to be interrogated."

"You have been. You may be again. Associating with people like that."

"They're not 'people like that' as you put it, they're . . ."

He interrupted brusquely. "Brothers and sisters under the skin, is that what you're going to say? For pity's sake, Maeve, bring your common sense to bear. You're not in their league, you stupid woman! You're the victim of cockeyed, idealistic notions. Not a criminal. Stop putting yourself on their side all the time. It was obvious in the radio interview. One of your 'friends' sent you a CND emblem drawn with blood. Remember?"

"A maniac."

"Possibly. Don't slip into insane behaviour now just because you happen to like your so-called friends. How often have you seen them?"

I told him. All of it. The departure of Walker and so on. If I hadn't, I guessed the police might. Or other neighbours less kindly disposed than the colonel.

He was appalled. "You have allowed these people on my property . . ."

"Our property . . ."

"Deceived me for several months . . ."

"Deceit is not my personal prerogative . . ."

"What is that supposed to mean?"

"I'm not sleeping with Oliver. I don't know what you're doing with Sarah."

That brought him up sharply. "Is that what you think?"

"I don't know. You have your freedom. I have mine. I can talk to Oliver and Rene better than to anyone else. I can stop them coming here, if that's what you want. But I won't stop seeing them."

We seemed to have reached an impasse and were both very tired. We sat opposite each other, not speaking for a while.

He said at last: "I don't want any harm to come to you, Maeve.

I feel you're walking straight into disaster, and I don't know how to stop you."

"You say that because you don't know Rene and Oliver. You've type-cast them. You refuse to see them any other way. And so do the fuzz. They sniff around Oliver – and Rene – and me. It's the way they operate."

He gestured impatiently. "The police are on our side, yours and mine. Your weird associates are distorting your judgment – and the way you speak. That radio presenter, Macbarra, put a question to you about prison corrupting. Your answer, as I remember it, was that there were no special breeding grounds for corruption. I can't think of any other breeding ground more likely to spread the virus. You asked him if tolerance could corrupt – obviously you had it in the back of your mind that it could. Well, it can. Take my word for it."

"So you think I'm corrupt?"

He winced. "No. Just foolish. Vulnerable. If you're wise you'll stop seeing the Dudgeons. But you're not wise, are you, Maeve? And I can't force you to be."

A passing car splashed the uncurtained windows with light. He went over and drew the curtains. We are in our safe, neat, little world here. Over on the other side of London Oliver is with Rene. Not so safe, perhaps. Not so neat.

Why did he go off so abruptly on his motorbike? He said he would wait for me, so why did he go?

9

For most of Saturday I lounged in a deckchair, half asleep in the very warm sunshine after a sleepless night. Christopher, his energy unimpaired despite his not having slept much either, was examining the contents of the shed. As ours was one of the few unburgled houses in the area, he'd hinted before making a start, what better repository could there be for stolen property? Dumped on me, of course, without my knowledge. After thanking him drily for his faith in my innocence, I'd suggested he might count the trowels while he was at it. There is a fine edge between anger and hysteria and I was precariously balanced between the two. I wish he would just put his arms around me sometimes and try to understand what I feel.

I feel fear of the police.

When I saw the two officers walking around the side of the house and into the back garden my throat went dry. It's an irrational response, but I'm not rational. They represent power. The power to incarcerate. When I can forget the smell of prison, the taste of it, the sound of it, then I'll greet them as fellow human beings.

They greeted me quite pleasantly and introduced themselves.

The spokesman, Sergeant Miller, is rotund, pink-cheeked, cheery-looking, the kind of bobby who does community work in schools. His side-kick, a young WPC, has a cut-glass accent and reminds me of Sarah.

Christopher, his hands filthy after messing around in the shed, acknowledged them with cold courtesy and listened to what they had to say. They wanted me to accompany them to the police station so that Inspector Grange might clear up one or two matters. He wouldn't keep me long. It sounded like a request, not an order, but I wasn't deceived. Christopher, in the kind of voice that brooked no argument, informed them that he'd come as well. They seemed indifferent.

He went upstairs to wash his hands while I fetched a woolly cardigan. The day no longer seemed hot. We met again on the front step and he put a restraining hand on my arm as I was about to go over to the police car. "We'll follow in our car."

The sergeant made no objection.

I thought, as we drove, how pleasant it would be if Christopher would, for once, step over on to the wrong side of the divide and point our car in the opposite direction. I felt strait-jacketed, as I sat beside him, and it wasn't all that easy to breathe. He glanced sideways at me, his expression stiff with disapproval, and asked if I was working up to an attack of asthma – and made it sound like a mortal sin. Another one.

I told him I didn't know.

"You've done nothing to be afraid of, Maeve. Apart from behaving like a lunatic befriending the Dudgeons. Don't tell the Inspector more than you have to. Leave most of the talking to me."

He should have learnt from past experience that the police don't operate that way. When we arrived he was told politely, but firmly, to wait in the reception area.

This local police station is very upmarket. Not at all like the one in Langdon where I was taken after attacking Sergeant Sutherland. The floor here is tiled in imitation marble and dotted around with potted plants. When I was in prison I found it helped my breathing if I focused on the unimportant. Now, I focus on the plants. Cacti. Mother-in-law's tongue. They don't help much. I follow the WPC down a corridor to a small, neat, brown-carpeted office where Inspector Grange is waiting. She introduces me, then goes through to an adjoining room, more of an annexe, where there's a table with a computer on it, and gets busy with some papers. The connecting door is left open.

The inspector is about forty. He is tall and bony and his wrists extend too far out of the sleeves of his navy blue suit, and the cuffs of his shirt are frayed. His tie is maroon with a small design of crowns on it. He wears his dark oily hair parted low to hide the bald area. He has a strong, closely shaved chin.

He doesn't call me Mrs. Barclay, the name I was introduced by, he calls me Maeve . . . And it's not an attempt to be pally. He's unpolished. Rough of speech. He's polite enough, however, to offer me a chair opposite his at his large, untidy desk and waits until I'm seated.

There's a tube of mints on the desk next to the telephone. He helps himself to one, then passes the tube to me. "Can't offer you a fag – given them up. Want one of these?"

I don't, but it seems ungracious to refuse. God, ungracious not to eat a mint! What's wrong with me? I accept.

He is observing me, his eyes, the colour of weak tea, are keen. "Bothered about coming here?"

"No, why should I be?"

"In the normal way you'd be finished with all this."

What's normal? But I know what he means. I don't answer.

"I wouldn't have asked you to come now only we're lacking certain background information. It's possible you might provide it."

"I don't know what you're talking about."

"Naturally not," it's spoken testily, "eventually you might. If you do, I hope you'll behave like the upstanding citizen you once were, so I'm told, before you clobbered my good friend and colleague." His smile is vulpine. "Ever heard of a snout, Maeve?"

"Yes."

Snout. Grass. Informer. I could produce a thesaurus of criminal terms if I had to. It's the sort of thing you pick up when you're inside.

"Can you put a name to this one?"

91

He produces a mug shot of a middle-aged man with heavy jowls. His neck is strongly muscled, or goitrous, the eyes protrude slightly. The face is vaguely familiar, but it takes me a moment or two to realise it's the man Sutherland was waiting for.

"I think it's the person Sergeant Sutherland met in the park."

"You're referring to Anselm Gardens where you spoke to Sergeant Sutherland yesterday."

Not a question. He knows all about it.

"I don't know what the place was called. This man came as I was leaving. I hadn't seen him before. I don't know his name."

He regards me thoughtfully, obviously wondering if I'm lying. "You're sure?"

"Quite sure. I'm sorry I can't help you."

"In this instance, Maeve, you're not helping me, I'm helping you. He has been known to the police, under all his aliases, for years. A useful contact for us. He digs up the dirt. Knows where to look. Makes his own messes, too. He's been inside a few times."

All right, I think. One of Oliver's less salubrious acquaintances. Oliver didn't thrust him at me, just made use of the information he'd given him about Sergeant Sutherland.

"He's been seen at a few anti-nuke demos in the past, before we got more pally with the Ruskies. Not that he was burning with zeal for a lily-white world full of angel song. In short, not on your side. Not on anybody's. A moocher along the edges of everything, ears flapping, eyes wide. Sure he's never approached you? Never bothered you?"

I think of the bloodied CND rag and am sure of nothing. I shake my head mutely.

"So it wasn't he who told you about Sergeant Sutherland?"

"No."

"You just waltzed along there, quite by accident. And bingo, there's the man you wounded, where you went to bend your knee. A good act of contrition, was it?" It's deeply sarcastic.

I'm silent. Even my mind is silent. There's a greyness inside my head.

He sighs. "Let's do a quick re-cap. What shall we call the snout? Chummy? Yes, that will do. Chummy meets Sergeant Sutherland. So do you. You don't know Chummy. Chummy doesn't know you. But Chummy knows somebody else. So do you. Chummy tells somebody else. Somebody else arranges it. Plausible?"

I don't answer.

"Enigmatic silence – is that the word – enigmatic? Okay. Your business how you got there. Our business if Chummy gets up to his tricks – a little blackmail – a nasty letter. If that happens, tell us. We'll run the little blighter in so fast he'll think he's got a rocket up his arse. Got the picture?"

He helps himself to another mint. "Well, *have* you?"

"Yes."

"Good. Want another of these?"

"No, thank you."

"Then let's get on." He puts the mug shot aside and produces another. "Have you seen this chap before?"

It's of a younger, thin faced man with high cheekbones and a lot of thick hair growing low on his forehead. Not bad looking. Again vaguely familiar.

He's aware of my hesitation. "Know him?"

I mumble that he looks a bit like my bank manager.

"What?"

I say it louder.

He's amused. "If you want your bank manager to give you a mortgage, or a nice fat loan, don't repeat to him what you've just said to me. He won't like it. This one got put inside for something no nice upstanding bank manager would do. He's been out some while now. Presently goes under the name of Hawkins. Heard of him?"

The question is ridiculous. I remind him that I served my time in a women's prison not in Wormwood Scrubs.

He grins. "Okay. Point taken. But those Chornley cons you lived with for a while have connections on the outside. Tell me if you've heard of – or seen – any of these. They've all served time."

He shows me several more pictures from his rogues' gallery and sketches in the background, all of it black. His attitude mirrors Christopher's strongly and he's backing it up with fact. Ring the leper's handbell. Unclean. Unclean.

93

I deny knowledge of any of them. In the pre-Chornley days all this would seem funny. It's not funny now.

"When you were inside did you get particularly pally with any of the inmates?" He misinterprets my expression. "No, I'm not asking you if you're gay. Just pally." He takes a photograph from his desk drawer. "With this woman, for instance?"

I'm expecting to see a picture of Rene, but it's a mug shot of Anna. Mug shots aren't flattering but you can't disguise good cheekbones and well formed features. And you can't disguise the expression in the eyes. Dazed, bewildered Anna, looking at the police photographer as he clicked away, feeling perhaps as I had felt. Finger printing I could accept as a minor assault on the flesh, but the mug shot lasers through your last shreds of dignity. Gotcha, Maeve! Now and for ever.

He's waiting for an answer. "I knew Anna, but we weren't particularly pally, as you put it. She was a shy, quiet woman. Kept to herself most of the time. She was released a couple of months before I was."

"Did she tell you why she had been put inside?"

"No."

He didn't enlighten me. "Did she have any family photos in her cell – room – whatever it's called in that progressive establishment?"

"I never at any time went into it, so I don't know."

He gestures at the photograph. "Would you say she was a good-looking woman?"

An odd question. He must have some reason for asking it. "Surely that's obvious."

"Oh, yes," he says drily, "quite obvious." He fingers the edge of the cardboard that the photograph is stapled to and then puts it down on the desk. There is more than a hint of anger in his voice, but it's controlled. "She doesn't look like that any more."

"What do you . . .?"

He interrupts brusquely. "She got herself carved up. Head and facial injuries. Her body was found dumped in the Euston area last Thursday – hidden behind a rubbish skip at the bottom of her back yard – a very trim yard, apart from the skip. Lots of flower pots painted white. Blood on some of them.

Trail of blood from the back door. She'd been out there a few days."

The room is too hot. Airless. Anna's crimson moorland is bleeding into my mind. Make it go. Concentrate on the grey monotones with the dark little house in the distance. Blot the whole lot out if you can. Anna. Beautiful, silent Anna. Clean, unbloodied Anna.

His voice is less rasping. "Bit of a shock. Are you all right?"

"Yes." I'm not, and he knows it. He gives me a few minutes before carrying on.

"It's usual for a woman to talk about her family. Did Anna ever mention hers to you?"

I moisten my lips, and try to concentrate on what he's asking me. "No. She hardly ever spoke to me."

"What about the other women? Any of them get closer to her?"

I think of the lesbian, the only one I'd noticed who'd tried. And Rene who was naturally friendly with everyone. But close? "I shouldn't think so."

"You don't seem sure."

"When she wasn't doing the usual chores she painted pictures. Usually on her own. That's all I know." Poor Anna. Poor lonely Anna.

"She never showed you any family snaps – group pictures – that sort of thing?"

The notion is bizarre. Anna would no more show snaps of her family to me than I would show snaps of mine to her. Rene, more gregarious than either of us, had been equally reticent. Even secretive.

"No, I've already told you . . ."

"Yes, yes, yes, you've told me. But sometimes when the memory is jogged you come up with something. Think. Gossip amongst the cons about her. Anything. Take your time."

A fly is buzzing against the window, trying to get out. He gets up and opens the window. The fly panics and takes the wrong route and finishes up on the ceiling. He looks at it with exasperation and then comes and sits opposite me again. "Well?"

"Sorry. There's nothing I can tell you."

"Have you ever run into her anywhere since your release – seen her around?"

"No, that would have been very unlikely." And then I think of Rene and realise it wouldn't. If I had met Anna, what would I have done? Crossed the road? Looked the other way? Probably. Rene is different, the friendship is unique.

He takes a mug shot out of a manilla envelope and passes it across to me without comment. It's the face of a middle-aged man with a receding hairline, a short fleshy nose, and well formed lips. You don't smile in mug shots, but he looks as if he could. Very easily. And sardonically. What the *hell*, you can imagine him saying, *is* all this? He obviously wasn't intimidated by the police photographer, or by his surroundings. It would be easy to imagine him on the other side of the cell doors, carrying the keys. That was the first impression. The anger behind the facade showed in the eyes and took a moment or two to register.

Inspector Grange is watching for my reaction. "So you haven't seen Horden before?"

"What? Who?"

"Reg Horden. Anna's husband. They both stood trial for the same crime. He's out on parole and he's done a bunk. We want to speak to him."

"You're telling me that Horden . . . Anna's husband . . . is the one who . . .?" The word 'murder' refuses to form. It's sickening to think of it.

He doesn't answer.

The two mug shots are too close to each other. I touch Horden's as if it's coated with slime and move it a few inches away from Anna's. It's a futile, protective gesture. I can't bear to look at her and think of what he's done.

Inspector Grange, aware of my action and obviously guessing the reason for it, takes Horden's mug shot and puts it on his side of the desk on top of the envelope. Anna's he lets stay.

"Most murders are domestic, but the obvious answer isn't always the right one. When we track Horden down we'll know more." From an assortment of pens, pencils, paperclips, in a tin on the desk, he selects a well sharpened yellow pencil and draws a circle on a scribble pad. Inside the circle he draws two Xs.

"Husband and wife. Centre of the domestic scene. Hell of a lot of aggro when things go wrong." He draws another circle surrounding the first. "Close members of the family. Another disruptive area. Especially ex-spouses and in-laws. We're trying to get all that background filled in. And then there's the third – the outer circle." He draws it. "Associates – workmates – the criminal fringe. The mug shots of those other ex-cons I showed you could be connected with Horden – or Anna – or both. I didn't just fish them out to show you the kind of murky water you could be dabbling your toes in."

He puts the pencil down and leans back in his chair. "You haven't been singled out for questioning. The other inmates who knew Anna will be questioned, too. If you'd broken all links with Chornley you'd have been further down our list. Most women like you, put in for your sort of crime, break those links pretty damn quick. They're so bloody glad it's over, they pretend it has never happened. In time, when the publicity ends, most of their upstanding, law-abiding friends – the charitable ones – pretend to forget it has . . . And talking of publicity, what papers do you take?"

It seems a complete change of direction. "The *Guardian* and the *Telegraph* during the week. *The Times* and the *Observer* on Sunday."

"Of course. Why did I bother to ask? Do you know what a tabloid looks like? Small square thing you can read in the tub?" His smile is sour. "Get hold of the tabloids tomorrow. They'll splash the details about Anna. But not all. We're doing a house to house in the area; neighbours notice who comes and goes. We may be getting somewhere."

The fly leaves the ceiling and alights near Anna's photo. He watches it morosely for a moment or two, waits until it moves closer and then tries to cup his hand over it. It buzzes angrily and moves off. He notices my expression of horror. "Don't be stupid. I wasn't going to squash it on the mug shot. That poor woman's had enough blood on her already."

He stands up. "Okay. That's all for now. If you can think of anything that might cast light on Anna's murder – come back. Or if you're uneasy – worried about yourself, for any reason –

come back. Policing is a two way business. We're here to help, too."

He precedes me over to the door and stands by it with his hand on the knob. "Just one last piece of advice: you won't like it, but you're getting it anyway. When life seems bloody boring and you want to liven it up, there are safer ways of getting kicks than by riding pillion on a powerful motorbike – especially if you're not sure of the bloke who's driving it. Until you are sure, Maeve, have a care."

He looks at me gravely for a moment or two and then, when I don't answer, gestures impatiently and opens the door.

The WPC comes out from the annexe and escorts me down the corridor.

On the drive home Christopher wanted a detailed account of the interview. I softened it up as best I could – no mention of the rogues' gallery – but you can't soften up murder. He could tell I was distressed about Anna and stayed silent for a while. His anxiety showed in his driving which is usually careful. After being hooted at for going through an amber light, he sighed deeply, then swore.

"Sorry, Maeve."

I'd heard a rich range of expletives in Chornley. They didn't bother me.

"Why question you about it?" he asked when we were almost home, "that's what I can't understand. Why question you?"

"They're questioning everyone who knew her."

"But, damn it, that will be the whole prison population of Chornley."

"Yes. It's called 'being thorough'."

"Once you touch pitch . . ." he began. Stopped. "I didn't mean that."

"Yes, you did. They're not all pitch. And my hands aren't dirtier than anyone else's."

"I didn't imply . . ."

"Yes, you did. Could we just shut up about it?"

Inspector Grange's last remark had got me on the raw. He hadn't mentioned Oliver by name. And there hadn't been any mug shots of Oliver on his desk. If there had been he would have spelt out his accusation word by vicious word. Therefore it was a vague generalisation, a warning with no substance. Motorbikes are dangerous. So are some drivers. *So what?*

"Prejudice," I told Christopher, as he turned the car in at the gate, "is the mouthpiece of a puny mind." It sounded like a proverb.

He told me coldly I was being offensive.

On Sunday when I suggested getting the tabloids in addition to *The Times* and the *Observer* he wouldn't hear of it. "Whatever appalling attack that woman sustained, it has nothing to do with you. So why upset yourself more by reading a lurid description?"

I was in no mood to argue with him, so made an excuse about driving over to the dairy to pick up a bottle of milk, which we needed, and stopped at the newsagent's on the way. Both the *News of the World* and the *Express* carried the story.

Kids Find Body was the *News of the World*'s caption under a photograph of a very young-looking Anna. This was followed by a brief paragraph:

The mutilated body of Mrs. Anna Horden (35) was found last Thursday evening in the backyard of her home in Lanyard Street, NW1. Two eight year old boys, Larry Stevens and Peter Wilmot, who were playing in the back lane, had climbed over the wall to retrieve their ball when they saw what they described as 'a lady asleep near a rubbish skip'. The police are anxious to contact Anna's husband, Reginald Horden, recently released on parole from the Scrubs.

The *Express* treated it differently. *Who Cares?* was their eye-catching and very disturbing caption:

How is it that a woman can lie dead for three days or more and not be missed? Are we so uncaring, these days, so unaware? Mrs. Anna Horden (35), brutally murdered and left to lie exposed to the elements in the garden of her neat little home in Lanyard Street, near Euston station, was last seen alive on the afternoon of August 21st., over a week ago, when she went shopping for groceries. A quiet woman who kept to herself, was the general comment of neighbours who seemed to know little about her. A sad reflection, perhaps, of modern society where 'keeping to oneself' is all too common. It is to be hoped that the police investigation will produce quick results.

As I folded the papers and put them in my canvas holdall where Christopher wouldn't see them, it occurred to me that the fact that Anna had recently been in prison hadn't been mentioned. Policy of the editors? Or had the neighbours, far from being uncaring, been extremely discreet? Inspector Grange had said the details would be splashed – they hadn't been. The only new information I had, apart from her age and address, was that two little boys had found her. That she had been discovered by children worried me. Mercifully they had thought she was asleep.

Christopher looked quizzically at me when I returned, rather late, with the milk, but didn't comment apart from reminding me that he was committed to playing in a golf tournament in the afternoon so lunch shouldn't be delayed. I made a cold one – ham and salad. Afterwards he insisted that I should go along with him and watch – to 'take my mind off things'.

Sarah, I noticed, was amongst the spectators and I carefully avoided her. After seeing Christopher fluffing some easy putts I went back to the club house and sat on the verandah with a Campari soda. Ours is a privileged world, his and mine, but in many ways puerile. He sets great store in plopping a little white ball into a hole and winces with annoyance when he misses.

He also sets great store on my safety, despite his relationship with Sarah, whatever that relationship might be.

Our marriage, like most marriages, is a confusion of emotions. I wonder about Rene's and Oliver's. It can't be perfect, no marriage is. Rene is not a biddable wife. Nor am I. But apparent compliance is sometimes better than conflict. Christopher won't tolerate having Oliver on the premises. All right. So be it. I will meet him and Rene elsewhere. But they have to be told.

How, for God's sake? *How*? And *when*? Difficult encounters are better faced quickly – so make it tomorrow.

As I drove over to their flat on Monday afternoon I played over the scene in my mind and couldn't get it half-way polite, let alone kind. I tried it with Samantha taking Rene's role, a futile exercise, but calming. "You're not wanted around, Samantha, Christopher doesn't approve." "Oh, shit, darling – why?" "You're socially and morally a sub-species, apt to contaminate our hallowed ground." Samantha, secure on both counts, would smile blandly and assume it to be a joke. A tasteless one, but nevertheless intended to be funny.

There would be nothing remotely funny about trying to tell Rene. So lie. Say something about Walker coming back, or a new gardener that Christopher has employed. Put the onus on him where it belongs.

I had only driven to the flat once before and it took me a while to find it again. As I took a couple of wrong turns and had to reverse out of a cul-de-sac I noticed a blue Ford Fiesta which seemed to be kerb crawling – or tailing. If the latter it wasn't very professional. The fuzz do it better, and the other lot should. Absurd imagination. A lost driver in these squalid streets, like me. I slowed down for him to pass, but he crept into another side road. Well, maybe it was a she . . . not near enough to tell. Not important.

Despite misgivings about the reason for my visit, I was eager to see Oliver again and find out why he'd left me so abruptly. Let him be all right. His reason needn't be a good one. Just let him be all right. *Please*.

I was talking out loud to myself. The other part of me that listened, and tried to console, didn't succeed.

There was an ambulance parked outside Rene's and Oliver's flat. I suddenly felt very cold as if the skin of my face had frozen.

10

Rene's face, as she is carried out on the stretcher, is barely visible, but the tangle of red hair is unmistakable. I park the car as near as I can and run down the street towards her. Someone amongst the small crowd of neighbours who have gathered on the pavement says something about an accident – a fall downstairs. "Into someone's fist?" is the riposte. I push them aside and reach her just before she is lifted into the ambulance. And am appalled. There are dark patches along her cheekbones where capillaries have ruptured and oozed. Her eyelids, half closed, look thick and heavy and are beginning to swell. Congealed blood has caked around her nostrils and her bottom lip has split. The angle of her jaw seems wrong. I reach out tentatively towards her but am afraid to touch her. She looks crushed. Broken. "Rene, for God's sake, what's happened to you?"

She tries to open her eyes and squints up at me. "Maeve?" It's a whisper but relief at seeing me is obvious. She is pain ridden, but aware.

The young woman ambulance attendant answers for her. "She says she tripped on the top step on the way down from her flat." Her scepticism is barely concealed.

"The heel of my shoe broke – I keep telling you." She moves her head awkwardly. "Maeve, Wayne is with old Ma' Heaton. Bottom flat. I gave her your phone number – for you to come and fetch him. He'll be okay with you until something is sorted out. You'll have him, won't you? Just for a day or two?"

"Of course."

Her world had exploded into violence. I would have promised her anything.

"Is there anything else I can do for you? Shall I come with you to the hospital?"

"Just see to Wayne. Get him away from here. Don't let anyone stop you."

"Rene – what about Oliver? Shouldn't he be with you now? How shall I contact him?"

"Not – your – problem." The words are forced out hoarsely. Her lower lip has started bleeding again and the ambulance attendant wipes it with a piece of gauze.

I begin seeing Oliver in a different light, but refuse to accept that the distorted vision might be the true one. He wouldn't have done this to her.

Would he?

For Christ's sake, no!

I was trembling when I rang the bell of the bottom flat. Had I been more composed I don't believe Mrs. Heaton would have let me in. She shuffled to the door in beige carpet slippers, a small, thin, hawk-nosed old woman wearing exaggeratedly large tortoiseshell-framed glasses through which she peered at me with deep suspicion when I told her who I was. She hadn't phoned Mrs. Barclay yet, she said, so how was it I'd come here so fast? Chance, I told her, I'd happened to be on my way. And could I have a drink of water, please, I felt a little sick.

"So you're not from the police?"

"No."

Belatedly she stepped aside and gestured towards the small front living room to the right of the hall. It smelt of lavender water which was probably an air-freshener of some sort. All available surfaces were covered with memorabilia of the Royal Family from

Victoria to the present day. She brought me water in a George the Fifth mug which had a chipped rim, but I drank from it gratefully.

She stood watching me, her back to the net-curtained window, her fingers plucking restlessly at the folds of her grey crimplene dress.

"This neighbourhood, madam," she said, "wasn't always like this. When I came here first it was quiet – respectable."

The 'madam' had slipped out naturally, but took me by surprise. She was about seventy, I guessed, and had probably been 'in service' as it was quaintly called half a century ago.

I let the comment pass and asked where Wayne was.

With her niece, Sharon, she told me, a couple of doors down the road. Luckily he had been there when his mother was attacked.

"Attacked?"

She made a little hissing sound through her teeth. "If she said she fell, then she fell."

"But you don't think so?"

"It don't matter what I think. I'm brewing up tea. Better than water. I'll pour you some."

It was an excuse to get out of the room, to avoid having to answer questions she didn't want to answer. But there were certain things I had to know and I followed her to the kitchen.

"Where's Oliver, Mrs. Heaton?"

She was busy at the sink. "How should I know?"

"Have you seen him today?"

She washed two cups under the tap, dried them, and put them on a red enamelled Silver Jubilee tray. "Milk and sugar, madam?"

"My name is Maeve. Maeve Barclay. Milk, please. No sugar." I watched her pour the tea and then asked it again. "Have you seen Rene's husband today?"

Her reply was enigmatic. "Husband? How do I know who I've seen?"

"I'm talking about Oliver."

"I know who you're talking about. The police were here yesterday. They did a lot of talking, too. With Rene."

"They've spoken to me as well."

"Maybe so, madam, but as a prison visitor. Not like Rene. That girl has made a mess of her life."

104

Had I not been so upset about Rene I would have been amused by the carbon copy deception. Rene, in my mother's eyes, had been respectable. I, in Mrs. Heaton's, wasn't an ex-con. It seemed wise not to disillusion her. It was necessary that she should let me have Wayne.

"We're friends," I told her. "That's why I'm here. I just want to help."

She carried the tray to the living room and put it on a small table covered with a blue chenille cloth. Then handed me a cup.

I accepted the unwanted tea and took a few sips. "I'll need to get in touch with Wayne's father," I told her. "I have to know where he is."

She was still suspicious of me. Very cagey. "Does he know where you are?"

"Yes, of course. He and the family have been to my home lots of times. And Rene gave you my telephone number, remember. Are you on the phone here?"

"I use the kiosk at the end of the road, like Rene."

"Do you think you might see Oliver later on today?"

She fingered the brown beads she was wearing, rubbing her calloused thumbs over them as if they were worry beads, or a rosary, and it was a little while before she replied.

"Perhaps, madam. I don't think so. But I don't know."

I felt I was in a wasteland – a limbo of non-communication. She knew a great deal more than I did, but was afraid to say too much. This could be out of loyalty to Rene, and perhaps to Oliver. If Wayne was fond of her, trusted her, then obviously she was fond of him. At her age to care for Wayne while his mother was in hospital would be onerous. She must surely be relieved that Rene had passed the duty to me.

Duty? The word had sprung to my mind and I didn't like it. Compassion – yes. Friendship – certainly. But put the word 'duty' to Christopher and he'd hit the roof. He'd hit it anyway, but that wasn't my present worry.

I told the old woman that I'd take great care of Wayne and make him as happy as I could. "But it would help me if I could know for how long. Speaking to his father would make everything clearer."

She took this as a statement and agreed with it but had nothing practical to suggest.

I asked her if she had found Rene, wherever it was she'd fallen. "Was it out in the hall. Near your door, perhaps?"

She said she hadn't found her. One of the neighbours passing along the pavement had heard her moan. "The outside door was open. She saw her lying there and went to help."

"She?"

"Mrs. Boscome. She serves at the corner shop."

"And was it Mrs. Boscome who sent for the ambulance?"

My questions were making her edgy. "I don't know who sent for it. Somebody came for me at Sharon's. Nobody wanted the little boy to see his ma' looking like that. That's why I didn't bring him back with me."

"And Rene didn't tell you anything, apart from asking you to get in touch with me?"

"No. She couldn't tell me much. Not in her state. Just what she had to say about fetching you for the little lad."

"Did she give you the key to her flat?"

"I already have her spare key. She has mine."

She allowed me to borrow it so that I could pack a few things for Wayne.

The upstairs flat looked extraordinarily neat. If Rene had been attacked then her injuries had been professionally inflicted. Her struggle had been minimal. Was it possible that she could have fallen downstairs, as she had said, on her face? It was the less distressing alternative and I tried to believe it.

On a stool by the fireplace was a stack of Oliver's motorcycling magazines and on top of them was the *Mirror*. There might be a more detailed account of Anna's murder in that – comments from the police, perhaps – more news of Horden, or anyone else they might be looking for. I got as far as picking it up, but couldn't bear to open it. Rene's pain was enough.

I had come to pack clothes for Wayne, so get on with it.

He had a lot of toys in his bedroom, but his clothes were sparse. And then I noticed a small holdall on his bed. It was full of a week's supply of little boy's clobber, including a sponge bag shaped like a bear. Rene, before her accident – accident? –

106

had planned to take him somewhere. On a holiday? With Oliver? Without him?

I opened the door to their bedroom. And saw chaos. The unmade bed was piled high with the contents of drawers. A suitcase upended on the floor had spewed out an assortment of underwear – all of it hers – most of it new. Tights, rolled in a ball, looked a peculiar shape. I picked them up and felt something hard inside. A small gold watch with a price tag still on the back. Two hundred and fifty pounds. A leather travelling clock with a mother-of-pearl dial had been ripped out of its case. It was unpriced. Obviously expensive. Obviously nicked.

So this was why he had done it. I remembered his words about a custodial sentence. Rene's insistence that the toy dinosaur had been my present to Wayne. Her explanation when she'd refused to take back the clothes that Oliver had returned to me – something about staying in one piece.

Her wounds had been brutal.

I can't equate what I've just seen with Oliver.

I can't accept this.

I can't bloody breathe!

I sat for a while until my lungs began to function more normally and I was able to think. The police had been here already, questioning Rene. Obviously not about shop-lifting or they would have arrested her. About Anna, then – her background, her associates – as they had questioned me. But if they came back and saw all this . . .?

They mustn't see it.

Macbarra's words about corruption started buzzing about in my head. All right – so I'm corrupt. So – where's her scissors so that I can cut off the price tag on the watch? I couldn't find them, so tore it off. Perhaps it was legit. Sold with the price tag on. Don't be stupid. You don't keep a watch in tights, you keep it in a drawer. So put it in a drawer, together with all the other stuff that has been scattered around, an odd assortment of not very expensive looking jewellery, perhaps honestly come by, perhaps not, and frilly underwear in cellophane bags.

Tidy the room up. Put everything back neatly. Make it look normal.

I had got it into some sort of order when Mrs. Heaton came up to tell me that her niece had returned with Wayne and that he was downstairs waiting for me. She eyed the bedroom shrewdly. "You put it straight."

"Yes."

Her lips were pursed in disapproval, but I sensed relief too.

She told me she'd found Rene's nightie and her washing gear while the ambulance was on its way. "It wouldn't do for nobody to come in here."

I agreed.

"Have you looked in the bathroom, madam?"

I wished she wouldn't keep calling me that. It made me sound like a whore-keeper. I told her once again that my name was Maeve and that I hadn't looked in the bathroom. What would I find there?

"Wayne's small lavatory seat," she said, "and rubber to put on his bed."

She showed me where the rubber sheet was kept in the cupboard with the spare towels and then picked up a towel that was folded on the side of the bath. There were spatters of blood on it. If Rene had merely fallen down the stairs there would be blood in the hall, nowhere else. Unless the ambulance attendants had come in here, used the towel and put it back again.

She was aware I'd seen it. "I'll wash it, madam. After you've gone. It's what Rene would want."

Yes, I thought, feeling sick again, she wouldn't press charges, no matter what.

I asked her if any disturbance, like this, had happened before. Disturbance – a bland, etiolated word, totally inadequate.

She answered obliquely. "Rene's a kind girl – but stupid. Do anything for anybody, but never no good to herself."

And Oliver, I thought, how do you rate him?

She re-folded the towel and put it inside the bath with the clean side up. Then she answered the question I hadn't asked.

"The little lad's had a rough time in the past. Someone abused him. Oliver got him right. Well, nearly right. That's my test of

108

a man – if he's good to a child, there's not much bad about him."
She began fiddling around with her beads again, almost clutching
them for comfort.

Not much bad. Or any bad at all? We might be jumping to
conclusions here. But for Christ's sake someone had hurt Rene.
And if not Oliver – then who?

Persuading Wayne to come home with me wasn't as difficult as I'd
feared. Mrs. Heaton had paved the way a little by saying that his
ma' had fallen down and had gone to hospital to be made better.

"Your mummy says you're to stay with me for a night or two,"
I chimed in, "until your daddy fetches you."

I watched for his reaction and he seemed calmly accepting.
Obviously no fear of Oliver.

"Won't that be nice?" Mrs. Heaton urged.

His solemn eyes regarded me and then he smiled.

He was sitting at the table playing with pieces of red and white
Lego. He had made a tank. It was quite intricate and required a
certain amount of dexterity.

"Present," he said. He looked at Mrs. Heaton and then he
looked at me. The gift was intended for one of us, he wasn't
sure which. After a moment's thought he got down from his
chair and gave it to me.

"Super," I said. And kissed him. He didn't draw back.

Mrs. Heaton, slightly huffed, came down to the car to see us off.

It wasn't until we were almost home that he mentioned his
mother. "Rene cut her knee," he said, "again."

Calling her Rene surprised me – the 'again' worried me. This
once silent child had discovered how to speak to me. It would be
easy to probe, but perhaps unfair and unwise.

"She'll be okay," I told him. "Knees get mended. She'll be
home soon. Everything will be fine."

It takes a lot of straws to break the average marriage. Ours,
in many ways, had borne a greater onslaught than most. This
particular straw, I guessed, would have a shattering impact, but
there wasn't much I could do about it.

Wayne was tucked up in one of the twin beds in the guest room when Christopher arrived shortly after seven. I had planned to break the news to him as gently as possible over a pre-dinner drink and hadn't reckoned that nature would force him to make a swift visit to the bathroom first.

He came down to the sitting room looking puzzled. "Maeve, why the small lavatory seat on top of the other one?"

I explained that it was a child's seat, and that without it the child would fall in.

"What child?"

I fetched the gin bottle and poured a generous amount before topping it up.

He repeated the question.

I handed him the glass. "A friend's little boy. His mother had an accident this afternoon. She had to go to hospital. I'm looking after him."

He put the drink down. "Who are you talking about? Fiona's youngster? What's his name? James?"

"No."

"Then who?"

I began stringing names together in my mind. Clarissa's Benedict. Charlotte's Gregory. Victoria's Paul. And then, just to gain time until I felt calmer, I wandered into the classical field. Clytemnestra's Orestes. Hecuba's Paris. Thetis's Achilles. Achilles with the vulnerable heel. And my weakness was what? Not being able to stand up for myself, my beliefs, without causing chaos.

He was waiting for an answer. "Rene's Wayne," I said.

"Reenswayne?" He frowned, puzzled. "What are you trying to say?"

I separated the words. Explained. Until now I hadn't mentioned that Rene and Oliver had a child. "He used to visit here with them. He trusts me. Likes me. I couldn't refuse to take him."

Christopher usually looks a little tired after a day's work, but he doesn't look drained. Now he did.

"You mean this woman – this Rene – landed you with the kid – in a matter of minutes – just before she was taken off to hospital? That you brought him here – without thought – without question? That he's actually upstairs now – in bed?"

"Yes."

110

I went and sat down. His untouched drink was on the small mahogany table by the chair. I sipped it. When does a youngster become a kid? At what stage of the social divide? It seemed an interesting question and I voiced it.

He told me to stop talking rubbish. "Keep to facts. What obligation have you to these people, or think you have, to be lumbered like this?"

"You're lumbered," I said, "or you're caring. Again we're into semantics, aren't we? It's all a matter of . . ."

His face was flushing with anger. "Shut up, Maeve. If you can't justify your crazy actions without being offensive, then stop trying. I don't give a cuss what social class your so-called friends come from. It's the criminal aspect I can't take. And don't start bleating about being an ex-con, too. I've had my fill of it. Where is he? Where have you put him? Not in our bed, I hope?"

"Naturally not. He's in the guest bedroom. I'll sleep in the other twin bed tonight. If he wakes up, he'll need to know I'm there." (And if you wake up, Christopher, you'll be so relieved I'm not.)

He strode over to the door and I followed him, alarmed. "You're not going up to the bedroom, are you? I've only just got him off to sleep. He's not five yet, for God's sake, a baby. If you walk in on him . . . frighten him . . . he'll . . ."

"I won't wake him."

Together we went upstairs and stood by the bedroom door. I had left the landing light on and Wayne's head was just visible, half covered by the duvet. He had taken a fancy to the crystal swan soap-holder in the bathroom when I'd bathed him and it was on the pillow beside him together with the Lego tank he was 'keeping safe' for me.

I watched Christopher looking at him and wished his face would soften just a little, but it didn't.

We went downstairs again.

"Why was he landed on you? Why didn't his father take him?"

"He wasn't there."

"Where was he?"

"I don't know. Rene wasn't in a fit state to tell me very much."

"If you hadn't arrived — so opportunely — who would have taken responsibility?"

I told him about Mrs. Heaton.

He didn't like anything I was telling him. 'These people', he implied, lived in 'their world' which was a thousand light years from mine. They had families, friends, to call upon at a time of crisis. To give a neighbour my telephone number in order to thrust responsibility upon me was a gross trespass.

"They've battened on you, Maeve. You're a soft touch, and they know it. Have you ever given them money?"

"No. Never." I told him about Oliver's reaction to the clothes I'd bought Wayne. I didn't tell him about Wayne's delight tonight when I'd dressed him in the pyjamas with a train on them. The clothes, until now out of sight in the suitcase on top of the wardrobe, would supplement what Rene had packed in the holdall.

He said, drily, "Your suppressed maternal instinct seems to have affected your brain."

"If the child upstairs was the son of a different mother, would you say that?"

He ignored the question. "Which hospital has she been taken to?"

"Whichever hospital serves the district, I suppose. I don't know."

"You don't know much about anything, do you? She is driven off into the wide blue yonder to one of a dozen or more City hospitals. Her absent husband, presumably unaware of what is going on, is to collect his child. You don't know when. Christ, Maeve, there are times when I despair of you."

Mutual, I think. But don't defend myself.

The casserole which had been put to re-heat on top of the stove began to give off pungent fumes of burning. I went to try to save it and then suggested to Christopher that we should eat. I had already laid the table and opened a bottle of good quality Riesling in the naïve hope of softening him up. Neither of us had any appetite as we sat at the table and he had no conversation. About anything. As always when under stress I began to babble, the words falling like flak in a war zone. My bright (offensive) comments about the state of the nation – finance – the Dow-Jones average – the weather – were listened to in icy silence.

Eventually he pushed his plate aside. "You can't even produce an edible meal."

"There are biscuits and cheese on the sideboard. Unsullied."

"I have to make some phone calls."

He went to telephone in his study, out of earshot, and was gone some time. I imagined a posse of police coming to remove Wayne – or an army from the DHSS breaking down the door. But he would be phoning Sarah, of course. The sane lady who was predictable, never unnerving, who soothed and smiled and had aspirations via his bed, and other beds, to great and glorious heights.

When he returned with an overnight case I wasn't surprised.

"Make sure to pack chocolates," I said, "the lady loves Milk Tray."

"What?"

"Beware Greeks when they come bearing gifts. Beware lovers when they come bare of gifts. They might just be making use of you. My friends make use of me when in need. I give gladly. You go to Sarah; may she receive you with joy."

He said bluntly, "You're drunk." It wasn't quite true, I was more sober than I sounded. I would have finished the Riesling if Wayne hadn't been upstairs. It was necessary to show some restraint.

Christopher's restraint was commendable, given the provocation. He told me that he had been phoning the hospitals. Rene Dudgeon was in Bart's and was likely to be there for a few days. He had been unable to elicit any more information.

"If you don't hear anything by tomorrow, Maeve, I suggest you contact the hospital. The telephone number is on my desk. There's a social worker, I believe, whose job is to deal with domestic problems. In this case your problem. Not mine." He went on to tell me coldly that it was impossible for him to remain in his home under the circumstances. It was asking too much. He couldn't behave towards the child (he stressed the word child) with the kind of tolerance the child deserved. The child had done no wrong. He would return at the end of the week, on Friday evening. If the father hadn't removed the boy, or the mother hadn't made other arrangements, then he would

113

report the matter to the suitable authority. In the meantime I was to take reasonable care of myself. He hoped the word 'reasonable' was understood by me, but he doubted it.

I promised to mug it up.

As I walked down the hall to the front door with him I asked him where he could be contacted.

"At the office by day, naturally. After office hours phone Eric."

"And he'll pass on the message to you at Sarah's?"

"He'll pass the message to me." Not an admission. Not a denial. I didn't press it.

The house felt strange after he had gone, as if emotionally vandalised. I had been given a present of silence and didn't like it very much. His departure, I understood, was necessary. Given his nature, the situation he had been thrust into was intolerable. His four day ultimatum was intolerable, too, but typical. It would never occur to him to comfort me – to tell me that I had done what I had to do – that Wayne was a nice little lad and that together we'd look after him until his father picked him up. Are there marriages like that? Utopian? Serene?

I imagined him spilling out his grief to Sarah. She would disrobe and succour, her cold green eyes implying that this time I had flipped my lid. I played the scene in my head as I washed up and was maudlin enough to weep a little for him. Had she been someone else, warmer, nicer, I might have wept for myself.

He phoned me at ten o'clock to remind me to bolt the doors.

I told him I already had.

11

At twenty minutes past two Wayne shook me awake and mouthed the word "wet" in my ear.

I could hear the rain sleeting down the window and the wind moaning softly.

"Raining," I answered sleepily.

"No." His voice was louder and he enunciated every word with extreme clarity. "I am wet."

I came properly awake. It was a declaration without shame, or fear, which was good. A nuisance to be dealt with as his two kind and loving parents would have dealt with it. I did everything that they must have done many times and blessed Mrs. Heaton for reminding me to take the rubber bed sheet.

Wayne spent the rest of the night in my warm, dry bed and I went back to the marital one which was cold and too big.

As I dropped off to sleep again I reassured myself about Oliver. If battering your wife is a regular occupation your child gets to know about it. This child is moving out from the silence of trauma because his home background is normal. He hasn't recently been frightened.

But he was off the premises when it happened.
And Rene warned me to get him away.

I phoned the hospital in the morning. Rene had had minor surgery on her jaw. She was comfortable. I asked if she could speak to me if the phone was brought to her bedside and was told it would be a couple of days before this would be possible. My query about her husband visiting her was parried by the nurse, sister, whoever was at the other end of the line. Was I a relative? she wanted to know. A friend, I told her. I don't know whether discretion or a need to get on with her job prevented her from telling me anything about Oliver. She suggested politely that I should speak to Rene later on when she was better – in the meantime did I have a message for her? "Tell her Maeve and Wayne send their love," I said.

If I hadn't been responsible for Wayne I would have taken flowers to her at the hospital. I couldn't leave him and I couldn't take him. She had kept very quiet about him when she was in Chornley in case the Social Services got their hands on him. This would apply to the hospital authorities, too, perhaps. Not perhaps, but almost certainly, if Christopher, failing to find anyone else to dump him on, deposited him at his mother's bedside.

I put a call through to Interflora and ordered a dozen red roses for her. Wayne wandered into the study while I was phoning and I asked him what message he wanted to send his Mum. "Tell her it's raining and I haven't a mack," he suggested after thinking about it.

"Tell her you send love and kisses," I said. "She can't get out of bed just now to shop for you. I'll get you a mack."

Having full charge of a child is very different from being one of a trio when the other two are parents. When he visited with Rene and Oliver he played in his own private world, murmuring to himself and paying us scant attention. Now, just the two of us, we were thrown on each other's company. I was afraid he would miss his mother and cry, so set out to entertain him all the time. I read more Beatrix Potter books to him – drew pictures with him with coloured pencils – showed him how to make pastry cut-outs. Talked all the time. Talked too much. Got on his nerves and he on mine. In the afternoon we both sat in front of a children's programme on the television and fell asleep. Exhausted.

On Wednesday the relationship was easier. The sun shone and he was able to play out of doors. When he came in for elevenses he reminded me that I'd promised to get him a mack. I pointed out that it was fine and that there was no immediate need. He pointed out that it would rain sometime and that if we went to buy it in the wet he would get wet. That he should express himself so lucidly, after such a long period of saying very little in my company, was heartwarming. Oliver had told me he'd spoken a lot about me, but it had been difficult to imagine.

It is difficult to imagine where Oliver is now and why he hasn't contacted me.

"If we go out to the shops," I told Wayne, "your daddy might phone and we won't be in to speak to him."

"He'll phone again," Wayne said. This child's calm confidence in his father abates my worry a little. His mother must have fallen. For God's sake, try to believe it.

We went shopping for the mack on Thursday after I'd done a little gentle probing about his reaction to crowds. Individuals, I discovered, he might regard as a threat, but people en masse were acceptable. He enjoyed being on the bus and wasn't too bothered by the shoppers in Oxford Street. The woman who sold us the mack was large, bossy and dominating, and he cowered from her. I whispered to him that I didn't like her either, but the shiny yellow mack was pretty super, wasn't it? He agreed it was. Lunch in the large restaurant of one of the stores he enjoyed – mainly because I told him he could eat what he liked and didn't fuss when he refused the vegetables. He was halfway down a large chocolate ice-cream when his attention was diverted by someone. He put his spoon on the plate and watched, smiling hesitantly. "A rabbit," he said.

I looked over my shoulder. "What do you mean – a rabbit?"

He was too entranced to answer.

There was a family with two young children immediately behind me. They were arguing over the menu. To their right four middle-aged women in hats were obviously out on a shopping spree. I could hear drifts of their conversation about bargains in the linen department. A haggard young woman with metal ear-rings large enough to distort her lobes was shovelling her way through a mound of curried rice.

"A mouse," Wayne said.

It was then I saw the small, fair man with a half-grown, scruffy-looking beard, seated alone at a corner table. He had taken two of the stiff white paper serviettes from their container and was twisting them into animal shapes. For Wayne's benefit. Obviously.

I had a feeling I'd seen him before somewhere. One of Inspector Grange's mug shots had resembled my bank manager. This man looked like someone I'd met at the BBC when I'd done the broadcast for Macbarra.

Aware that I'd noticed him he came over to our table.

"Hello, Maeve."

It *was* Macbarra.

He smiled at my astonishment and fingered his chin. "A combination of necessity and vanity. A shaver's rash and a longing for a neat Vandyke. It might improve. If I don't appear too disreputable, may I join you?"

"Of course."

He pulled out the third chair, moved some of the cutlery aside, and put the two animal shapes in front of Wayne. "A rabbit and a hamster. The rabbit is easier to do. I'll show you how."

He went through the stages of folding the paper, and then guided Wayne's hands as he had a go, too.

As I watched them my eyes burned suddenly with tears. Why couldn't Christopher have shown Wayne just a little warmth, a little acceptance? Macbarra, a hard-bitten professional interviewer, who hardly knew me, was being kind to him.

He spoke to me as he helped the child. "I didn't know you had a son."

I answered thickly, not quite in control emotionally.

"He's Rene's little boy. She was my friend in Chornley."

And now recoil, I thought. Behave as Christopher would. Get up and go. But please don't. He's happy with you. Smiling at you.

He looked directly at me then, aware perhaps of the strain in my voice. "May I order you another coffee?"

I accepted and he ordered some for himself, too.

"I was a bit bothered about the interview, Maeve. How did you react to the broadcast?"

"It was endurable. Just."

"You could have written me a caustic note."

"What would be the point?"

"You might have felt better for it. Accept my apology now. What I have to do doesn't always please me."

"But you have your audience to entertain."

He agreed he had. "And from that point of view, the broadcast was by no means a disaster. According to audience response, quite the reverse. The so-called success stories I'm working through at the moment won't be rated so high. Inarticulate artists – deaf authors – stammering scientists. All right – so I'm exaggerating – but not much. At least you were able to say what you thought needed to be said."

"And you took most of it out," I reminded him.

"The policy of the powers that be. And some protective cover for you, too, believe it or not. It isn't always wise to align yourself with the losers." He glanced at Wayne, seemed bothered by what he'd said. "Don't get me wrong. The comment was intended in a wider context."

Wayne had picked up his spoon and was eating his ice-cream again. The paper rabbit he'd made was propped against the water jug and he kept smiling at it with pride. Macbarra took his ballpoint out of his pocket and handed it to him. "Try sketching in its eyes so it can look back at you. No, laddie, put it flat or you'll knock the jug over."

He watched him for a few minutes, made encouraging comments, and then turned back to me. "Have you got a job yet? Or perhaps you don't want one?"

I thought of Sarah. "I haven't been offered anything suitable. And recently I haven't been looking. It's easy to get used to doing nothing."

"I can't imagine you sitting back for long. It's a waste of your talent. How is life treating you – generally?"

An oblique reference to Christopher, I think. I tell him everything is fine.

A useful word – fine.

By the time the coffee came we hadn't a lot to say that could be said in front of Wayne. Eventually, however, he made a careful

119

reference to Chornley again. "Past events are probably difficult to forget, but do you feel easier now? Less uptight? Most of the time, during the interview, you had me on the edge of my chair."

I confessed I was as uptight as ever. "It's not just difficult to forget, it's impossible. Something awful happened to someone I knew there. She'd been out a few months . . . and . . . well . . . she . . ." I glanced at Wayne. "I can't be more explicit, but the fuzz wanted background information from the cons who'd been in Chornley with her. I had to go down to the local nick, mostly to look at mug shots, including one of her before she . . . well . . . before . . . not one of her afterwards, thank God. And there was one of her husband. I wasn't able to tell them anything of any use. I hardly knew her. It happened in the Euston area. You may have read about it."

"You're referring to the woman who was found by a rubbish skip – the one whose husband's on the run? Harden . . . Horden?"

"Yes. Horden. Anna Horden."

"According to a piece about it on the telly last night, he's still missing. And there's another bloke they want to interview, apparently he and Anna . . ."

Wayne, suddenly losing interest in the rabbit, interrupted him. "Anna?" he said. "Where's Anna?"

Startled, Macbarra and I looked at each other and then back at Wayne. After a moment or two he seemed to forget the question. "The rabbit," he said, "should have whiskers."

There is so much I don't know and perhaps will never know. There are many Annas in the world. Motherly matrons – pig-tailed little girls – storybook Annas. And one murdered Anna, whom his parents would never have told him about. A name that appealed to him, that's all, surely? It can't be significant. I wondered what Macbarra had been about to say about the fuzz nosing after someone else, but it seemed wise to drop the subject. Wayne's presence was inhibiting.

Before leaving us Macbarra duly admired Wayne's new mack-intosh which he insisted on putting on to show him despite the heat of the restaurant. "A friendly little lad," he said quietly to me as Wayne struggled with the buttons.

"With you," I said, "with me – and just a few more." I chose the words carefully. "When the world is inimical – and in his case, it has been – it takes time for confidence to grow. Quite a long time. Thanks for helping the process. He's had fun with you."

"And I with him. It has been good meeting you, Maeve. I hope everything goes very well for you in the future." He helped Wayne with the top button. "There's just one thing wrong with this splendid yellow mack of yours, laddie, the buttonholes are too darned small."

Wayne smiled at him. At ease. Very happy.

It was four o'clock when we returned home and the phone was ringing. I made a dive for it but was seconds too late. Damn, oh bloody damn! It could have been Oliver.

In the quietness of the house I am aware of passing time and pressing problems. Tomorrow evening there will be a confrontation with Christopher if Oliver doesn't come. Christopher is within his rights if he refuses to harbour Wayne. I am within my rights, as joint owner, to insist that he stays. And so the marital home is rent in two. Wonderful ambience for the child.

If the battle has to be fought it had better take place on neutral ground. My mother's caravan will one day be mine. If my heels have to be dug in, they'd better be dug in there.

I asked Wayne if he would like to have a day or two beside the sea – starting tomorrow. "Unless your daddy comes for you this evening."

He was watching Tom and Jerry on children's television and didn't seem too bothered either way. I wondered if he had been there before. Probably not. Oliver hadn't had the key very long.

At seven o'clock when I was running his bath the phone went again. Without waiting to dry my hands I rushed to the extension in the bedroom and picked it up. It went dead immediately.

It rang for the third time at two-thirty in the morning. I was dreaming I was climbing up a gaunt, black rock into a grey plateau of ash when Wayne shook me awake. "Not wet," he mumbled sleepily. "Bell."

I picked up the receiver in the dark. Whoever was at the other end was still there. Oliver? Christopher? Not Christopher. He

121

would phone me by day. "If you're ever on your own at night," he told me once, "and the phone rings, don't answer with your name or number. Just wait." Would Oliver understand my caution? Would he think Christopher was lying beside me in bed – or holding the receiver?

"I'm not wet," Wayne said loudly. "But I will be soon. And I can't see in the dark."

There was an audible gasp at the other end of the line – a suppressed chuckle – and the caller hung up.

I felt a thrust of quite irrational fear. It wasn't Oliver.

Instinct is a weird animal. You can't force it to conform to the dictates of common sense. How the sweet hell can you analyse a muted laugh when your brain is sleep-sodden and say it hasn't this characteristic or that? In the morning, as I sliced bread for the toaster, I tried talking myself out of my fear of the night-time caller. It could have been Oliver. He had laughed when he'd heard Wayne, as Oliver might have laughed. Could. Might. Anxious words. Instinct is more robust. You know without being able to prove it that whatever you feel at a particular moment is right.

I have a strong recollection of the man in Anselm Gardens. The snout of many aliases. The stirrer of mud who went running to the fuzz if he found anything useful. What had Inspector Grange said about him? A moocher in areas where trouble might brew. Not those words but near enough. A spy at protest meetings, including perhaps the one at Langdon. Had he been there watching me when I'd thrown the brick? His meeting with Sergeant Sutherland in Anselm Gardens, about something quite different admittedly, still indicates a link. Was he the creep who'd drawn that CND emblem in blood on one of his snotty pieces of rag? If so, is he still lurking around?

Could be.

Should I inform Christopher? Or the police? No, to both. I haven't seen him – not here. Just heard the voice. Then how about telling the colonel? He started the Neighbourhood Watch. But there's nothing definite to tell. An anonymous phone call and a laugh that made my skin creep. It's not enough. Unless it happens again. Please God, it won't.

Over breakfast Wayne informed me that he wanted Rene. This was a moment I'd been dreading, his sudden awareness of being bereft. I wanted Rene, too. I wanted her to come here in Oliver's continuing absence and take on her proper role as Wayne's mother. As a surrogate mum I wasn't brilliant. Half the time I did things wrong. Too much milk on his cornflakes. Lacing his shoes too tight, or not tight enough. Lack of authority when a crisp "no" was necessary, because I didn't want to upset him.

"If I can get her to come on the phone in hospital," I suggested, "would you like to talk to her?"

He said he would.

"Then eat your toast while I try to get through."

"There's too much butter on it."

I scraped some of it off.

The lines to the hospital were busy. Eventually someone answered and put me through to the ward.

A Sister with a warm cheerful Irish accent was on duty. Mrs. Dudgeon had contracted a mild infection, otherwise she was due for discharge today. The doctors were on their ward rounds now, so taking the telephone trolley to her bedside wasn't possible.

"Do you think the doctors will let her out soon – tomorrow, perhaps?" (*Let her out* – shades of Chornley.)

"No, but she might be well enough to leave by Sunday or Monday. I can't be definite. Try phoning after lunch, I might have more news for you then."

It was necessary for Rene to know where we were, but I had to get Wayne off the premises before Christopher came. "Would you tell her I'm driving down to Shuter's Cove this afternoon, to the caravan, and I'll phone her from the village when I get there, about five or six?"

She asked me to spell Shuter's Cove and I did so slowly. "Wayne will be with me," I added, "please be sure to tell her that."

Wayne, eager to speak to his mother, had come into the study and was listening. When he saw me replace the receiver he went back into the kitchen, picked up the sugar bowl and dropped it on the floor. Deliberately. He crunched his sandals in the mess. Looked at me, his face flushed and angry, his eyes suffusing with tears.

"God damn!" I whispered. I couldn't help it.

He ran over to me and held me around my waist, pushed his head against my jeans, and sobbed.

I stroked his hair until he had quietened down. "We'll phone your mummy from a phone box," I soothed. "It's an old-fashioned red one in a funny little village near the sea. The doctors are still busy making her well. Three or four sleeps in the caravan, and three or four days playing on the beach, and then you'll be home with her again."

He was trying to say something and I held him a little away from me so that I could hear him. He told me between gasps that his nose was running. This was obvious. I found him a tissue and held it while he blew.

He mumbled that he could blow it himself and that he loved me.

I got all choked up as well. Together we swept up the sugar and put it in the pedal bin.

Before leaving the house I wrote a note for Christopher: "I am taking the child to the caravan and he will be with me there until his parents collect him. The responsibility is mine. Please – please – please don't interfere. You could do more damage than you think."

The last time I had been to Shuter's Cove, Christopher and I had been trying to salvage our relationship. The weather, I remembered, had been bleak. The more upmarket attempt at salvage in Paris had been pleasanter as regards creature comforts, but marred by the nightmare.

In this present crisis I have to live from day to day and accept what happens. Caring for Wayne could kill my marriage, but it was dying anyway. On this lovely August afternoon, with the sound of the sea like faint cello notes in the distance, I feel less uptight than I did earlier in the day. We had quitted the house by eleven. All doors carefully locked. It's peaceful here in the village and the sea wind blows softly, ruffling Wayne's hair, pushing mine into untidy tendrils.

He keeps reminding me of the phone call to Rene.

Soon, I tell him. First we must stock up with tins of food before the shop closes. The caravan is basic. No fridge. And he will need a bucket and spade.

Together we carry parcels out to the car. He's enjoying this and is starting to have the holiday spirit. A kite, red and green and with a multicoloured tail, completes his pleasure.

It's five-thirty when we phone Rene.

She sounds very tired and is speaking with difficulty. The surgery to her jaw must be giving her pain. Her message to Wayne is brief but it must be loving and reassuring because he nods and smiles and says yes and tells her about his kite. He hands the receiver back to me and goes and waits for me outside. I tell Rene that he's out of earshot now – okay – but missing her.

"Has Oliver been in touch with you at the hospital?"

"No. He can't . . ." She mumbles something inaudible.

"Rene, I didn't hear that. Why can't he?"

". . . God-forsaken place . . ."

"What?"

"My damned jaw – pills helping, but not much. Why did you leave your house . . . why go to the wilds?"

"Because Christopher could be difficult. It's better for both of us in the caravan."

"Difficult . . ." Something else I can't hear.

"He's not good with children."

". . . short time . . ."

Not even for a short time, I think, if that's what you're trying to say.

"Maeve . . . dark . . . lonely . . . not good. Take him back home."

"You mean your home? But you're not due to leave hospital just yet. Unless Oliver is there?"

"No . . . wait a minute . . . drink." There's a pause. "Your home . . . not to my flat . . . not till I say."

I have to be honest. "Rene, Christopher isn't being supportive in this. If he had been I wouldn't have come here. I have to stay here until Oliver fetches him, or you're well enough to come yourself."

". . . not to anyone . . ."

"What?"

"Don't let anyone have him . . . keep him close."

125

"But surely nobody but Oliver would . . .?"

I can hear voices at the other end of the line and then the Irish nurse comes on. "Mrs. Dudgeon is finding the conversation stressful. It's not easy for her to speak. Just a moment . . ." I can hear her saying something to Rene and then Rene comes back on.

"Maeve . . . take care . . ."

"Of course. Wayne will be fine with me."

The nurse takes the receiver. "That's all for now, I'm afraid. More conversation in a day or two. Oh, and your flowers are lovely. I'm sure she'll want you to know that. Nothing nicer than red roses, and they've good long stems. Don't worry about her, she'll be all right soon. I promise. Bye-ee."

Bye-ee. A cheerful high note end to a disquieting few minutes. The old song floats into my mind. "Bye-ee. Don't cry-ee. Wipe the tear, baby dear, from your eye-ee."

The brief period of tranquillity has gone.

I had forgotten how dark the environs of the caravan can be.

I leave the phone box, and smile because Wayne is looking at me. He slips his hand in mine.

It's a ten minute walk from the coast road to the cove where the caravan is sited. As on other occasions I leave the mini in a lay-by and carry what I can. Last time Christopher carried the boxes of provisions and I managed the two overnight bags. This time it takes two journeys. Wayne has energy enough for the walk, luckily. He wants to know if there are hens in the farm he can see in the bend of the hill. I tell him yes and that we'll buy eggs and fresh milk there tomorrow.

The caravan is well placed for sun and doesn't usually get damp, but as I unlock the door I'm aware of the pungent smell of brine as if the place has been scrubbed out with sea-water. Or bleach. The main living area and bedroom are dry, but the blue lino tiles in the kitchen section are wet at the edges and fading off to grey here and there. In the past rain has trickled under the edges of the back door and the window frame has never fitted well, but the central area near the dining unit has never been damp unless washed. And when washed it was fresh and clean and smelled pleasantly of soap.

Wayne says something about "stink," which is rather an exaggeration, but I agree and open the window. Had Rene and Oliver been here, I wonder, and spilt something with a strong stain – like blackcurrant juice?

It's necessary to make sure that the bunks are aired, so I fill a couple of hot water bottles and put them in. Meanwhile Wayne pokes around the cupboards and drawers and exclaims at the 'funny' lavatory. Is a chemical loo funny on a second inspection or only when you see it for the first time? I ask him again if he's been here before and he says he's been to lots of places – that he went to Japan once and sat in a space ship – and that had a funny lavatory, too. You pressed a button and it took off. It takes too much energy to sort out facts from dreams and he's enjoying the latter, so why cast a blight?

For supper I heat up soup and a tin of ravioli, which isn't too revolting, and picnic with him outside where the grass is short and dry and crisply adorned with harebells. I tell him tales of my childhood holidays here and he listens sleepily. The evening is lilac and grey and the waves break softly on the darkening beach below.

There have been times in the past when being here was idyllic, or seems so in retrospect. Now there is beauty, but unease. Rene's anxiety, caught like a virus, can't be dispelled. The words she'd used – dark – lonely – God-forsaken – had been highly charged. To be in an emotional state after a battering is natural. But why focus on the caravan? And on Wayne? Kids are supposed to get the feel of a place; as far as he's concerned it feels all right.

How would he react if Rene took him to a women's refuge? I repress the thought. Oliver wouldn't have . . . but if he had . . . and more than once . . .? How much do you have to love a man to put up with that? Is there a streak of masochism in the women who do? Or do they stay together for the sake of the kids? If so, they aren't doing the kids any favours by keeping them in that sort of environment. Perhaps they stay for financial reasons. Can't afford to leave.

I take my financial freedom for granted. Rene can't. I don't know one half of what goes on inside her head – or Oliver's. I don't know much about their life-style either, apart from what I've seen. We were close in Chornley, she and I, out of need.

My need. And now I'm here with her child and glad to be, but with niggling worries I can't quell.

Wayne is tired and doesn't protest when I tell him it's time for bed. He has found something that looks like a piece of twisted brass — small — not much bigger than a toggle on a coat. It's a space button, he tells me, and wants to put it under his pillow like the Lego tank he forgot to bring. It isn't very clean, but he might miss his tank, so I let him.

In the night an animal comes prowling around the caravan, one of the farm dogs, possibly. It whines but doesn't bark and seems to be scrabbling as if trying to get at something under the van. It will tear its claws on the concrete base; there isn't even room for a cat under there. I think of rats and shudder. The luminous travelling clock beside my bunk points at five past three. A hell of a time. I wonder if I should get up and make myself a cup of tea. The light would scare off the dog, but it might wake Wayne. Better not. I lie wakeful and after a while the scrabbling stops. The silence is very deep and the darkness is thick like a bandage over my eyes. Sergeant Sutherland must have feared total blindness in the first few days after I hurt him. Had he lain in his hospital bed cursing me? Are any of the Langdon villagers finding it hard to sleep tonight, or does the nuclear pollution of their land worry them less intensely than it once did? In all honesty, my own feelings are no longer so acute. I did what I felt I had to do — then. A passionate action that didn't do any good.

Oliver's words at our first meeting come to me: *Our nuclear winters are leaking pipes and no central heating.*

Nuclear winter, before the real thing, is as cold and forbidding as this caravan feels tonight.

Wayne mumbles something in his sleep. It sounds like "Anna".

I slept eventually and in the morning everything seemed more normal again. My dark mood had passed. Saturday was bright and vigorous. The wind whooped in from the east and the waves crashed and brawled and tore into the shingle, shoving it up into blackly gleaming heaps. Wayne wanted to bathe, but saw the wisdom of waiting until the sea was calmer and was content to spend some time at the farm instead. These days a young couple are running it – Jean and Nick Corby. City types. She sculpts in her spare time. Her husband does a little carpentry, house names, garden furniture, wooden toys. They kept pigs for a while, Jean told me, but couldn't bear the thought of their bloody demise. Now, it's just free range hens, killed by someone from the village. And accommodation for summer visitors. More civilised. I had already heard most of this from my mother who always visited them when she was in the caravan, but I nodded and made appropriate comments while Wayne went to choose himself a present – a wooden owl.

It was obvious that the environs of the farm fascinated him – a playground for animals, enhanced with little white wooden houses. Nick explained that they were called hives and showed him a honeycomb. He treated the child with grave courtesy as he would a contemporary. Wayne, in his silent way, accepted him, provided I was near.

A recent innovation was a farm shop sited next to the dairy. Here I stocked up with butter, honey, eggs and milk, also ham and sausages from the deep freeze. All at city prices to support the rural dream.

Jean walked part of the way back with us and we stood together at the top of the cliff path leading down to the cove. Below us the roof of the caravan could be seen, shadowed occasionally by passing clouds. "It's a good situation for a family," she observed, "ideal for you and your husband, but not the best of places for an elderly person like your mother. She could be taken ill there and no one would know."

I pointed out that she always visited with friends.

"But they're elderly, too. I don't want to worry you, but . . ."

I waited to hear what she was reluctant to tell me.

She spoke hesitantly. "Nick and I were walking the dogs along the beach recently, fairly late. There was a light in the caravan. We knocked, thinking your mother was there. There was no answer. The curtains were drawn so we couldn't see in. Nick went down again in the morning. The curtains were open. There was no one there. The place seemed to be all right. Not vandalised, or anything. Was everything in order when you opened it up?"

Everything, I thought, except the smell and the wet floor.

I told her that some friends of mine had a key. That everything was fine. God, that word again! The more I use it the more twisted up I feel inside. When people knock on doors, you open them. So why hadn't Oliver – or whoever – done just that?

It started raining after lunch, a heavy downpour that lasted for about forty minutes. And solved the mystery of the wet kitchen. The wind was forcing the water through a small hole halfway up the wall opposite the window. The hole had been plugged with a pale grey adhesive substance and hadn't been noticeable until the adhesive loosened and the rain began trickling through. I remembered that Christopher had used a sticky substance in a tube around the leaking sink on our last visit and went to the tool box to fetch it. There was enough left to stop the flow of water.

Wayne watched while I pushed it in. "Chewing gum?" he asked.

"No. Chewing gum is hard to start with. This stuff is supposed to harden in the hole. And you don't eat it."

Wayne suggested that the hole might have been made by a woodpecker with a big beak trying to get in.

I couldn't think how it had been made. A hole in the roof would suggest a weakening of the fabric. A hole in this position was hard to explain. Wayne said he'd fetch his magic button. That would stop anything.

He came back with it and held it towards me on the palm of his hand. "Look."

This time, I did. Properly. And realised for the first time what it was. An empty cartridge case. Someone had been shooting rabbits or birds hereabouts. I asked Wayne if he'd found it out in the field.

"No. Over there, by a spider. The spider ran away." He pointed to a narrow aperture between the broom cupboard and the wall. A child could get his hand in there. No one else.

I asked him if he was sure. Yes, he said, he was.

It was hard to believe, but I believed him. The cartridge and the hole tallied.

Someone had fired a gun here in the kitchen and the bullet had gone out through the wall.

My breathing was beginning to go haywire as I tried to find a more acceptable explanation . . . and couldn't.

Somebody had shot somebody. *Here*.

The abominable bloody smell had been just that – blood. Only it couldn't be. Blood once washed away doesn't smell. But can you ever wash it away? Wouldn't it seep through the floor? Get down underneath? That dog was after something. Attracted by what – the smell of congealed blood?

For Christ's sake! Almost choking I went and sat on the kitchen chair, my feet in the puddle of water, and Wayne stood and looked at me and rubbed the cartridge case up and down the side of his pants as if he was trying to make the bloody caravan with its bloody bullet hole take off like his bloody Japanese lavatory into space and . . .

And . . .

And . . .

I rested my face in my hands and took long, deep, shuddering breaths.

12

Most things can be rationalised. It depends how badly you need everything to be normal. I ached for normality and began rationalising when my breathing eased. The hole in the wall could have been caused by many objects. Such as? Well – anything. It could have happened at any time in the past. Christopher could have repaired it when he'd repaired the sink. He wouldn't necessarily have said, "Look, Maeve, I'm mending a hole." All right. Agreed. Wayne said he'd found the cartridge case in the kitchen. He probably hadn't. Kids say what suits them. Rene's macabre comments about the caravan had upset me, but Rene is stuffed full of pills to stop the pain and not to be taken seriously.

And this shouldn't be taken seriously.

Blood?

What blood? I haven't seen any.

And so on . . .

And so on . . .

Over and over . . .

Soothing, palliative words which I only half believed.

By the time I was capable of getting up from the chair and

mopping the floor the rain had stopped and the sun was shining again in a watery sky. Wayne wanted to fly his kite and we went outside together to fly it, and lost it in a gust of wind, which upset him. His father, he said, wouldn't have lost it. His father would have held the string tight.

My feelings about Oliver continued to be ambivalent. Inspector Grange's insinuations had made me angry, but uneasy, too. Rene's broken jaw, the blood spattered towel in her bathroom, were sick-making memories.

He arrived when late afternoon shadows were beginning to form and for the first time since I'd known him I felt no pleasure, just a strong awareness that in many ways he was a stranger, a man who had his own life to lead, and in his own way, and who might or might not have battered Rene. Wayne, who had been playing with his wooden owl on the caravan steps with me, gave a whoop of delight when he saw him crossing the field and ran to meet him. Oliver picked him up in his arms and hugged him. Watching them together made me ashamed of the doubt that still lingered. There was love here. Gentleness. Surely he would hurt no one?

He looked very neat in grey cords I hadn't seen before and an ubiquitous white shirt and navy anorak. He was even sporting a tie in restrained shades of blue. He put Wayne down and came over to me. "It's very good of you to take care of him, Maeve. I can never thank you enough."

It was stilted. Almost a parody. I was reminded of the first time he had come to my home. Everything then had been 'very nice'. He touched my hand briefly in a gesture that was ridiculously formal. Despite the warmth of the day his fingers were cold.

I murmured something equally stiff about it's being a pleasure and glad to help. Wayne was prancing around us, his joy natural, his response unforced. Oliver and I watched him rather than each other. His proximity disturbed me, but not in the same sexual way as before. He seemed remote, despite his closeness, as if his thoughts were elsewhere.

He'd met Christopher, he told me. It was Christopher who had told him where to find me. "I'd called at your house, expecting Wayne to be with you there."

I tried to imagine the meeting. Christopher very stilted, his disapproval obvious. Or had he been downright hostile? Was Oliver's attitude towards me now the result of Christopher's attitude towards him?

"He offered to drive me," Oliver said, "but I had the van."

A polite encounter, then.

Christopher had probably gone back home to suss out the situation. A brief visit away from Sarah. He would be back with her again now.

Wayne was asking him about Rene. When would he see her?

"Soon," he answered vaguely.

"She fell and hurt her knee."

"Yes."

"Silly Rene – silly Rene – silly Rene," he chanted happily.

Oliver suggested abruptly that we should go inside the caravan and collect Wayne's things. "It's a long drive back. I don't want to leave it late."

I took him through to the kitchen and told him I'd fix something for him to eat first. "A fry-up. Ham and sausages from the farm."

He wasn't hungry, he said. He'd had a snack on the drive down. The drive had taken longer than expected. He'd forgotten to bring the map.

"Then you haven't been here before?"

"Once only. Shortly after you gave me the key. Wayne was recovering from chicken-pox and Rene and I thought a few hours by the sea might be good for him, but the place seemed to be occupied so we didn't come in." He sensed my bewilderment. "What's the matter?"

"Christopher and I haven't been here for a long time. And my mother is still away." I told him what Jean had told me.

"A couple of youngsters wanting to have it off," he suggested. "A warm caravan is better than a cold beach."

"But this was recently, and they'd used a key."

"Or a piece of plastic card. The security system in your home is rotten. This is worse. They've probably been making a habit of coming here. Have they nicked anything?"

"No."

"Done any damage?"

I glanced at the wall and he went over and examined it.

"Horseplay — kids getting rough. You're lucky it's repairable. A carpenter will fix it for you."

It was a neat re-writing of the scenario. Believable. I liked it. But that smell still lingered and I didn't like that at all.

Oliver asked if Wayne needed to be fed before they left, or had he eaten? He'd had a fry-up less than an hour ago, I told him. Wayne, overhearing, said he'd like a packet of crisps to eat on the beach. He hadn't used his bucket and spade yet, he complained, and didn't want to go home until he had.

Oliver agreed to give him an hour. "We'll build a castle together, a large one with a moat around it."

"And Maeve will play, too?"

"If she would like to, yes."

The wind had abated and in the slanting golden light the patches of wet sand glowed strongly amongst the pebbled area. The bay, one of many along the coast, was deserted. The misty blend of colours, soft shades of September, was like a Turner seascape. A memory of several months ago came back to me, my first sombre impression of Oliver as one of the immigrants in the Ford Madox Brown painting. A romantic concept when my mind was in flight from a situation I was finding it hard to adjust to — the stepping out as an ex-con into the world of the free. Later, the impression had changed. His laughter had been unforced, his vitality strong. Now the first image is back with me again — there's something about the eyes . . .

As the three of us helped to build the castle we spoke very little. Wayne was engrossed in the purely physical pleasure of scooping up the sand, patting it, shaping it. Oliver's thoughts obviously weren't with us — with Rene, perhaps, as mine were. This was a family scene and she should be here. He smiled at his child and sometimes at me, but mechanically and without warmth.

The castle built, Wayne began decorating it. He went searching for the right sized pebbles and shells along the line of shingle and Oliver and I, alone for the first time, walked together along the creamy edge of the incoming waves. He was wearing black lace-up shoes and I suggested he should take them off. "You'll ruin them."

"It doesn't matter. I haven't been back home to get changed."

"Why not?"

He ignored the question.

I removed my sandals and let the waves curl around my toes. The sea was sharply cold and I focused my mind on it, unwilling to think of his flat as I'd last seen it – Rene's loot flung around the bedroom – Rene herself . . .

"This is a pleasant place," he said, "you must have liked coming here as a child."

"Yes," I agreed. "Very pleasant."

Pleasant. Nice. Very nice indeed. Emasculated words. Our knack of communicating together, once so easy and happy, has suffered some kind of mental block. We're silent for a while. The silence hurts.

He breaks it at last to say he's been away for a few days. In Newcastle. "There's a possibility of a job there. And a house. A three-bedroomed terraced. Rene had agreed to come up and see it – before she – well, when . . ." He stooped and picked up a piece of seaweed. It smelt of iodine. Of hospitals. He flicked it into the water.

"You're wrong," he said.

"What?"

"You think I battered her."

"No!" The blood is rushing into my cheeks. I am ashamed. Abject.

He's unemotional. "So do some of the neighbours. We've had rows. Not when Wayne was around. Never then. The worst was about that toy dinosaur she nicked. Remember? She lied about you giving it. Wayne was in bed asleep and she was putting it away, and began lying again. I hit her. Open-handed. Not punched. She gave me a kick in the balls. Both sorry afterwards. The boy didn't wake up."

I don't know what to say. Christopher and I have been near to losing control, too, but never that near. We walk on in silence. A seagull swoops around as if life up there is amusing, no, more than that – frenetically joyous.

Relief makes me feel the same.

He waits for the gull's raucous screams to fade as it rides the wind into the distance, then carries on in the same dull monotone. "I used to have family on Tyneside. Was born and brought up there. Still have contacts. It's the right sort of move for us. Better for Wayne. Everything more settled. Regular money coming in. Cost of living not so high. A decent little house. Rene might keep her hands in her pockets for a bit. Not be tempted."

I ask him if he has been to see her in hospital yet.

"No. I phoned on the way down here."

"But why not visit?"

"I've told you – I've been away."

He blocks any further questions I might ask by describing the job offer. It's in a furniture warehouse, a new outlet for a firm specialising in hand-crafted beds, and sounds grey and dreary like a flock mattress. I feel like commiserating, but stop myself in time. Does he seriously believe Rene will stop shoplifting when he uproots her from London? And what will she fancy when she goes up there? The consolation of bright cheerful baubles or something more expensive? I'll miss her when she goes. I don't want her to go.

He cuts across my thoughts. "Will you spend the night here in the caravan, or will you drive home this evening?"

"I don't know. I haven't decided."

"I should think your husband would want you to go home."

I doubt it, but don't say so. Oliver is distancing himself quite deliberately. He and Rene. Christopher and me. Our hands brushed by accident just now and his tension was communicated in some weird way so that I, too, am disturbed. He seems to know this and walks a little apart from me.

The screen of words is up again. This time it's about Wayne's schooling. When he gets settled in a new home he'll have to start attending somewhere. Yes, I say, yes. We both agree he's bright. Well, he is. A few minutes of this and we can't think of anything else to say. He suggests we turn back and waits while I rub the wet sand off my feet and dry them as best I can on my handkerchief. My sandals feel gritty and uncomfortable. A drifting thin cloud sweeps a net of grey over the beach. The air is becoming cold.

Wayne, in the distance, seems small and frail as he plays in the shadow of the cloud. And then his playing stops and he is suddenly unnaturally still.

Oliver, with a father's instinct, is the first to realise that something is the matter. He quickens his pace, starts to run, then forces himself to walk quietly. Alarmed, I follow.

Wayne is crouching over a little mound of shells and pebbles he has collected. On top of them is a piece of driftwood, carefully placed. It seems to be concealing something. Something that frightens him. He hears us coming, stands and backs away, his movements are stiff and jerky, his face expressionless like a cardboard mask. Oliver takes him gently by the shoulders. "What's the matter? What is it?" The contact eases the child's rigidity and colour burns up into his cheeks. He reaches up for his father's hand. Tugs at it urgently. And then, his mouth tight with an effort not to cry, he lets it go and runs forward and kicks the driftwood away. Amongst the scattered pebbles and shells it has been covering are the remains of a man's black leather belt, sea-sodden. The clasp, made of metal, is in the shape of a butterfly.

I remember his phobia, how frightened he had been of the butterfly in the garden. His reaction then had been almost cataleptic. He had curled up on the grass like a child in the womb. Now he is standing very still, looking at the belt, his arms crossed in front of him, his hands clenched into fists. Oliver is touching him gently, his cheeks, his hair, and gradually he is relaxing. He picks him up and walks a little way down the beach with him, and then back towards me again. Not saying anything. Just holding him close. Oliver's face is dark with changing emotions that are hard to hide. Rage. Grief. Fear. And then he glances down at Wayne and I see only love. He carries him past me and up to an area of burnt gorse above high tide level and away from all the rubbish that the sea has piled up.

He sits there, holding him, rocking him, as if the little boy has regressed to babyhood. Then gently he releases him and puts him to sit beside him.

Distressed, I stand by the butterfly belt on the scattered stones, wanting to help, but not knowing how. Oliver becomes aware of me and asks me to bring the belt over to him. I hesitate. It doesn't seem wise. "Are you sure?"

He nods.

Wayne cringes as I approach with it and Oliver presses him close to him again. "It's all right. Finished with."

He takes a knife from the inside pocket of his anorak. The blade springs forward when he presses the hilt. A flick-knife. Small, obviously very sharp. He tells Wayne to sit a little away from him in case the knife slips. And then he gets busy with it, slashing the belt into small pieces. The metal clasp, hard and resistant, won't yield. He grinds at it, gouges it, more as a release of anger than with any hope of destroying it.

All the time the little boy sits silently beside him, never looking away.

"And now," Oliver says, "the sea can have it again."

He gathers up the pieces and tells Wayne to follow him. "Hold Maeve's hand."

His hand is cold in mine and he's trembling as we clamber up the rocks at the water's edge. It's treacherous here and we walk carefully to where the water is deeper. Oliver scatters the slivers of black leather into the sea where they float like eels and then slowly sink.

He holds the clasp out to Wayne. "Throw it in."

He shakes his head mutely, not wanting to touch it.

"Then we'll throw it together. Your hand on mine."

It seems necessary for it to be disposed of in this way, like being in at a death. The wicked giant shattered at the foot of the beanstalk. The wolf's demise in the boiling cauldron.

It's a clumsy dual effort, the clasp doesn't reach the water and has to be retrieved. The second throw takes it out into a gully where it drifts for a while on a bed of seaweed and disappears slowly.

"For Anna," Wayne says.

Oliver glances at me and then he looks away. "Yes," he says, "for Anna."

13

There were obvious questions to be asked but they had to wait until Wayne was resting in the bunk and out of earshot. I had heated up some milk for him and put a hot water bottle in beside him. He had stopped shivering and his eyes were heavy with sleep.

I suggested to Oliver that it might be better if they stayed the night. "You can have the top bunk, to be near him. I'll bed down on the sofa in the living room."

He said he'd rather go. "He should be fit for the drive a little later on."

I followed him through to the kitchen and he asked me if I had any beer.

"No. I just stocked up with pop and Coke for Wayne."

"It doesn't matter." He took out a packet of cigarettes and lit one with a match from a box on the sink. "Is this place insured, Maeve?"

It seemed an odd question – irrelevant – as if all that trauma down on the beach counted for nothing. I told him my mother had probably seen to it.

"You cook with paraffin," he indicated the stove. "Not very safe. You're careful, but intruders mightn't be. If an accident should happen, especially at night, it wouldn't be easy to get out."

I wondered if his reluctance to stay the night had anything to do with fire risk and couldn't believe it. There were two easily accessible exits. He was leading me down devious paths away from the main issue. I brought him back to it.

"Oliver, who was Anna?"

He was smoking nervously, without obvious pleasure, but with obvious need. I hadn't seen him smoke before, but the packet was half empty.

"You know who she was. One of your mates at Chornley."

"She was nobody's mate," I said, "except, perhaps Rene's. But what had she to do with Wayne? That belt reminded him of her. And he's mentioned her before."

"Has he? What did he say?" His anxiety was obvious.

"He just asked where she was." I told him about our meeting with Macbarra at the restaurant.

He relaxed a little. "So you took him out for a meal. Wasn't he bothered meeting someone he didn't know?"

"No. Macbarra entertained him. He enjoyed himself. He was calm and happy. But back there on the beach he wasn't. And you know why. So why prevaricate? Why not tell me?"

He looked for an ash-tray and failing to find one used a brown egg-cup from the crockery shelf. "Is the smoke worrying you?"

"Yes."

But he was worrying me more. The mug shot of Anna on Grange's desk. Grange's warning just as I was leaving. The obvious link between Oliver and Anna.

He opened the back door to let in fresh air and flicked ash on to the grass. "That better?"

I nodded.

Wayne stirred in his bunk and murmured in his sleep. Oliver glanced down the length of the caravan to the bedroom area and his face looked lined and suddenly old. "He got scared because he was reminded of something. The butterfly in your garden frightened him, too. Same reason. In time he might get over it. He won't ever forget."

I had unloaded all my troubles on to him in the past, my guilt

141

about Sergeant Sutherland, the nightmares, and he had consoled me. But what consolation could I offer him in a situation I didn't understand?

"What won't he forget? And what had Anna to do with it?"

"Does it matter what she had to do with anything? Now. It's all in the past. Finished with." There was an edge of anger in his voice. A warning off.

It seemed wise to heed it.

I made the excuse of the cigarette smoke to take one of the folding kitchen chairs outside. Let him follow me if he wanted to. Talk if he wanted to. Or keep on treating me like an importunate stranger.

Clouds were sweeping up into yellow banks along the horizon as if forming a far ephemeral shore. A slow moving container vessel was a long dark smudge against cobalt.

He joined me after a little while, carrying the other chair and my red woollen jersey. "Put this over your shoulders. It's chilly now."

The gesture was thoughtful. Oliver as he used to be. I drew it around me gratefully.

He told me he'd gathered up Wayne's things and put them in the holdall. "I remember those pyjamas with the trains on them. You've been a good friend to us, Maeve, but you've stirred a few rows."

"If I have, I'm sorry. I'm fond of Wayne. Of Rene. I want everything to go well for all of you."

He lit another cigarette, glanced at me, then stubbed it out. "Everything should go well. Now. If Rene doesn't get another custodial sentence, that is. Would you say she's a good mother to Wayne?"

The question surprised me. "Of course. She loves him. Cares for him."

"Has she ever spun you the yarn about a breech birth, or whatever it's called? How long it took for him to be born – her attempts to breast feed – and so on?" It sounded derisive.

"No." What was he getting at?

"What about our wedding, then? Full church service – orange blossom – the lot?"

"Yes, but not in that sort of detail. What are you trying to say?"

142

The tension was back in his voice, "I'm trying to say what I probably shouldn't say, but Rene might tell you if I don't. She gets bursts of honesty now and then. Anyway, there's no reason why you shouldn't know. You won't blab to anyone, particularly not to Wayne."

He leaned sideways in his chair and picked up the stubbed-out cigarette from the grass. Examined it. Put it back in the packet. Changed his mind. Threw it out. All his movements were nervous and totally unlike him.

"Anna," he said, "was Wayne's mother. She was my common-law wife for five years. When we split, I moved in with Rene. And left Wayne with her. Kids are supposed to be better with their mother, and he was only two at the time. This was four years ago."

It was startling. Unbelievable. Wayne was obviously Rene's child. He didn't look the least like Anna. And his age . . . according to Oliver he's going on for six, a year older than Rene told me. But when I'd bought him the clothes he'd needed the larger size. So Rene had been lying. But why?

"Rene's hair," I began, "and Wayne's . . ."

He cut across. "That's the only resemblance. There's red hair on my side of the family, it has skipped a generation. He has Anna's features – Anna's eyes."

Anna at Chornley – dark questioning eyes.

Wayne's questioning eyes before he'd learnt to trust me.

And down there on the beach as he had made that final gesture with the belt he had spoken her name. The destruction of something that had terrified him had been done not only for him, but for her.

I don't want to believe it.

But slowly I am believing it.

"Anna wanted him," Oliver went on, "like any natural mother would. And I visited often. Everything seemed okay. He was thriving normally. Happy. Until she married Horden and the bastard abused him."

His speech, staccato until now, deepened with anger. "No – let's say it straight – not use fancy words – he buggered him. Sodomised him."

He sat hunched in his chair, silent for a few minutes, as if blind to his surroundings. Remembering.

"I didn't know what was happening. The first few months of the marriage seemed okay, there was nothing obviously wrong. He seemed to be behaving all right towards Wayne, so I stopped being vigilant. I let a few weeks go by without seeing him, and I'll blame myself for that forever. He was my kid. My responsibility. Christ, he needed me. Anna brought him round to me one evening. Horden had battered her when she'd tried to protect Wayne – but Wayne had been hurt worse. I wanted to get back at Horden then – and should have – but she was scared witless of what I might do to him. And what he might do to her – afterwards. Later, when we were all calmer, she kept fobbing me off with talk of losing her home. Had he flung her out she'd have been lucky, but she didn't see it like that."

He became aware of my reaction and his voice softened a little. "If you feel as sick as you look, then I'm sorry. The first time Rene saw Wayne undressed – that night Anna brought him to us – she vomited. And then she started loving him, as you said, and mothering him. Better than his mother ever had. Anna came to visit – on and off. Wayne called her Anna, and Rene has always been Rene to him. Less complicated. We've moved around quite a bit – quit the district where he was known. He should have gone to school a year ago, but he wasn't fit and we managed to keep him away from the authorities. The neighbours where we're living now think he's Rene's kid. It's better for Wayne that they should. Later he'll have to be told. So now you know most of it, Maeve. One of the few who do."

Truth when it is resisted takes some while to sink in. The family picture had shifted out of focus and all I could see clearly was Wayne, the brutality he'd suffered, and the image was unbearable. Oliver and Anna, as a couple, I couldn't see at all. He didn't fit with that pale Madonna creature. With Rene, yes. Vibrant, warm Rene. It occurred to me that the two women in Oliver's life had both been in Chornley at the same time. What had Anna done? When Horden had stood trial for child abuse, had he dragged her into it, too?

144

I asked Oliver.

He shook his head. "I didn't report Horden. If I had, how long do you suppose it would have taken for anyone to act? And if they had got off their butts and started an enquiry they'd most probably have taken Wayne into care. They wouldn't see Rene as a suitable foster mother. Not with her record. Besides, I had to think of Anna."

"But you must have done something? You couldn't have let him get away with it."

He glanced at the caravan as if to make sure that Wayne was still asleep. "When my family is hurt," he said quietly, "no one gets away with it. But I do things my way."

He seemed to be debating whether to tell me any more or not. At last he decided to trust me. "You understand what I mean by a set-up, don't you? Crack was a possibility. It's comparatively cheap. Cocaine baked into crystals with baking powder and ammonia. You might have come across it in Holloway – smuggled in. Anna isn't . . ." he corrected himself bitterly, "Anna *wasn't* into drugs, but having them on the premises might have tempted her. I couldn't risk that. It had to be something else – something Horden would get his dabs on – fingerprints for the fuzz. Anna told me they were having some work done on the house, on the black economy, payable in cash. He'd drawn five hundred from the bank, mostly in tens. Swopping with counterfeit notes was easy. He'd paid some of it out before the fuzz were alerted. They searched the premises. Found wads of it. Anna should have kept her mouth shut – as she usually did – but this time she was so keen to have him put inside she said too much and got herself charged with him. I hadn't meant that to happen to her, but I couldn't do anything about it without getting my mates into trouble, as well as myself. And Wayne needed me. I was working for a haulage firm when Rene was put inside. I threw up my job to look after him. Couldn't trust him with anyone else."

Oliver's devious reprisal, with the help of his mates, shook me. Christopher's search for stolen property had been irritating, but I began to see things more from his point of view.

He resented my lack of approval. "The bastard had it coming to him. Anna was the unlucky one, but according to Rene she didn't take it too badly. Horden was shocked rigid. Never been in trouble before. Worked in insurance, or something respectable. The kind of bloke your lot would invite to bridge – or whatever games you play."

The sudden hostility in his voice was startling.

He apologised. "I'm not lumping you in with anyone. You're different. One of us. As much as you can be."

It was meant as a compliment, but it was hard to respond.

"Think of Wayne," he said bitterly, "and keep thinking about him. That belt on the beach – Horden had one like it. Pretty things, butterflies, when they're not made of metal at the end of a leather strap."

I felt cold and drew my jersey closer around me. There was a burst of bird song in the hedge at the bottom of the field. It was sweet, melodious, but didn't soothe me at all.

"Horden got a short sentence," Oliver went on. "Too short. First offence. A bit of doubt, perhaps. Had he been in the dock for sodomising Wayne, he might have got off altogether. A decent sort of chap, the jury would have thought, looking at him. Nice grey suit, tidy hair, polite way of talking. Not the kind to do that sort of thing. So let him go. Prisons too full anyway. I just did what I had to."

He was expecting me to say something, but I still couldn't think clearly.

"All right," he said at last. "I'm not expecting praise. Or blame, either. All I'm sorry about is that I didn't follow my instincts when Anna came round that evening with Wayne. And made a proper job of it then. If I had, she'd be alive today. Just before Horden was taken down to the cells he said he'd 'redress the situation' – his words. It didn't sound much of a threat, unless you knew him. In plain talk it meant getting back at those who set him up – starting with Anna. Some of the tabloids mentioned mutilation. She was slashed around the face and head."

He was opening and closing his hands in a pumping rhythm like a heart-beat. "If he'd got pulled in by the fuzz, stood trial for Anna's murder, and got sent down for life, how long do you suppose it would be? Ten years? A bit more, perhaps. And then he'd be let out. Same bloke. Same sodding, murderous bastard.

Just a bit older. You don't believe in topping, do you, Maeve? Too brutal. Not nice. That bit of violence that happened to Sutherland had you sweating in horror. Your world is all bright and shiny and false – the real one is rotten and hard and bloody. That day I took you to see Sutherland, the bloke who was meeting him told me about Anna – and that the fuzz were doing a 'house to house'. Neighbours had seen a red motorbike in the lane near her back gate the night before she . . . before it happened. I'd gone to check if she was okay, now that Horden was out on parole. I wanted her to move in with someone for a bit. Not be on her own. She was so simple minded she didn't believe he'd bother her again. Said the home was hers, legally, not Horden's, and she wouldn't leave it. Called it a nest. Oh, Christ, nest!"

He breathed deeply, trying to control the words that were tumbling out. "I keep seeing her – hair very neat – pale blue dress – sitting on her fancy new sofa while I tried to talk sense into her. She'd bought a matching rug – fancy flowers on that, too, and kept on looking at it, not at me. Everywhere very clean. Pale grey carpet. If he did it to her there there'd be blood all over – great stains everywhere. And on him. When she was found she was outside where he'd flung her like a dead animal."

He was almost weeping.

"And then . . . there was Rene. Horden got at her the day she was supposed to join me in Newcastle. I should have been with her. Everything happening the wrong time. Important to have a job. More important to get Rene away. But she was stubborn . . . like Anna had been. She'd things to see to, she said. Clothes to wash and pack. And Horden's target had been Anna. Not her. With the fuzz after him he'd keep out of sight for a bit, she believed. And so should I, she warned me. After all the questions the fuzz had been asking about Anna's family – and finding out I'd lived with her – they'd be sure to pull me in. So keep away. They'd pull me in all right, I knew that. And give me the usual tests – like they'd give Horden – blood, saliva, semen. It's routine. I'd be clean but they'd take time finding out. And I hadn't time to give them.

"She was getting ready to leave on the afternoon train when he walked in on her. Wanted to know where Wayne was. That

Wayne was the cause of it all. When she wouldn't say he pushed her into the bedroom and beat her up. He threatened he'd 'give the child a difficult time if she informed the police', his words again. The girl friend of one of my mates saw her in hospital and Rene spilled it all out to her. She kept me in touch with what was happening – including Rene's story about the 'accident' cover-up. Well, there won't be any more 'accidents'. If she's fit enough tomorrow, Wayne and I will go along to the hospital and take her home. And the fuzz can pull me in for questioning and take all the time they want."

His tension was slackening and the nervous movements of his hands became still. For most of the time he had been speaking at me, rather than to me, and the last few words seemed to be a thought spoken aloud and just for Rene. "It's over," he said quietly. "It had to be done."

At first I didn't understand the significance of what he was saying. It was when he turned and looked at me that I knew. There was supreme satisfaction in his face. A hard, glad rejoicing.

It had to be done.

His hands as they rest so quietly now on his knees look gentle. Well-shaped nails. Tranquil fingers. A killer's hands? An executioner's hands?

You don't believe in topping, do you, Maeve? Too brutal. Not nice.

There's a bitter taste of bile in my mouth and I swallow with difficulty. The setting sun is bright, dizzying, laced around with clouds. The long orange line of the horizon won't stay still. I close my eyes and am aware of my heart beating.

I hear him getting up and sense the heavy feel of his body close to me. He stoops and touches my cheek. I cringe away. His eyes, dark brown like Wayne's, are wary as he looks down at me. It's Oliver, I tell myself. Wayne's father. The man who shows tenderness to his child. Out there in his 'rotten, hard and bloody world' professional executioners are going about their business. And are paid for it. My mind, fending off creeping horror, is about to go on one of its absurd escapist flights into the ridiculous. The returning hangman greeted by his wife: have

148

you had a good day? I smile foolishly at Oliver then bite my lips to keep them closed.

He tells me to take it easy. I am. How much easier can I take it, for Christ's sake!

A dog comes trotting through a gap in the hedge. Its muzzle is sandy as if it has been digging for something. For what? It disgusts me. I shout at it to go away. It looks amazed, affronted, then slouches off.

"That belt," I say at last, as if I'm talking of a purchase at Harrods, a mildly interesting purchase, "was Horden's?"

He answers that they're mass produced in their thousands – not Horden's at all. A smooth lie. Necessary.

He is being very careful with me. Solicitous. How about going back to the caravan for a drink? he suggests. No g. and t. I tell him. Nothing of any interest. Only Coke. Or coffee. We decide on coffee.

He keeps looking at me rather oddly as I pick up my chair, fold it, and carry it up to the caravan. It feels as if the show is over, but in this weird theatre the audience takes the chairs home, too. What's the next move? Coffee? I set about making it.

He sits at the kitchen table. "Maeve."

"Yes?"

"I don't want you to see Rene for a while."

"Why?"

"Because you're not going to be very good for each other just now."

I spoon instant coffee into a mug, add hot water and sugar, and give it to him. "Why aren't we good for each other?"

"You have been good, very good." (A doctor tone of voice – the patient is ill.) "But you might badger her. Make her say too much."

I understand him, of course. Absolutely. He has said too much.

"The trouble with you," he diagnoses, "is the way you build things up. It was a million to one chance that a belt like Horden's was washed up on the beach. It was unlucky that Wayne found it. He'll forget it. So must you."

It's a command. He's sipping his coffee. Now he's smiling at

149

me, but his eyes are bleak. He points to my empty mug. "Make your drink, then we'll go and wake Wayne."

I'm about to do as he says, but my hand is trembling and my wrist touches the boiling hot surface of the kettle. A small area of skin becomes blotchy and pink. It's a slight burn, the kind you cope with. Only I don't cope. I stand and look at it. Oliver takes me over to the sink and puts my wrist under the cold tap, runs the water over it, dries it. Then he fetches the first-aid box, a biscuit tin, kept on the top shelf next to the spare crockery. There's a tube of antiseptic cream in it and he rubs some of the cream very gently into my wrist.

How did he know the first-aid kit was kept in a biscuit tin?

On the top shelf?

This is the first time he's been in the caravan . . . isn't it?

My mind must be shouting out the questions because he's receiving them loud and clear.

He looks away from me and replaces the tube of antiseptic cream next to a roll of bandage. A packet of gauze is wedged on the other side. He removes it and puts it next to a packet of lint. Unnecessarily. Fingers moving restlessly while he thinks. He has the sort of hands surgeons are supposed to have: capable, deft. What do surgeons use in operating theatres to mop up blood? Swabs? But if the blood flows from a gunshot wound on to the floor of a caravan and the stain is spreading . . .?

He puts the lid on the tin and replaces it on the shelf. "Odd place for a first-aid kit. I happened to notice it when I was collecting up Wayne's gear. Thought he might like a biscuit."

It's a feeble lie.

My bowels are feeling like water.

"Maeve, what's the matter?"

"Nothing, I'm . . . It's just that . . ."

I rush to the loo and sit there. And feel so sick . . . so sick . . . so sick.

Oliver tapped at the loo door after about ten minutes. "We should be going shortly. Wayne's awake." He sounded normal. Very calm.

I wasn't ready to face him yet, but I had to be. For Wayne's sake I had to be controlled. I splashed water on my face in the tiny basin, cooling my skin, and felt a little less nauseous.

Concentrate on ordinary things. Don't question Oliver about anything. Think of Wayne . . . all the time. He's the important one.

He was sitting on the side of his bunk and looked very sleepy. Oliver had dressed him all but his shoes, which he couldn't find. I found them under my bunk and put them on him. Wayne poked his finger down the side of his shoe and said his sock was wrinkled. I smoothed it.

All the while Oliver and I were carefully polite with each other, just saying what had to be said and avoiding eye contact, like strangers trapped in a lift between floors and aware of the long dark shaft below.

He lifted Wayne on to his shoulders and carried him across the field and down to the road and I followed with his hold-all. The van, parked in front of my mini, looked very clean as if it had recently been hosed. Oliver put Wayne down and told him to stand beside me while he arranged the travelling seat for him in the back. The van was very clean inside, too, as if it had been scrubbed. There was a faint tang of anti-septic.

He turned back to his child. "Okay – in you go."

Wayne backed away. "Maeve's coming, too." He clutched my hand.

I gently released it. "No, I'm going on later. In my mini. To my own home."

His eyes widened in dismay. "But you can't. You're coming with us."

Oliver interposed, "Maeve has been kind to you and looked after you very well. Now you must say goodbye to her."

He stood mute, his lips trembling.

I hugged him, but he didn't respond. "I want you to come. The three of us in the van."

"But who would drive my mini?"

"It would drive itself." He turned to his father. "I can magic anything. Make cars go. Make Maeve come. All I have to do is rub this."

He took the empty cartridge case out of his pocket and showed it to Oliver.

This was a scene I couldn't play, didn't want to watch, didn't want to know about. So turn your back on it. Walk away. There's no proper kissing goodbye to Wayne, now. There can't be.

I crossed the road and leaned against the wall. The cliffs below the headland were a purple grey in the twilight, remote, forbidding. There was a hint of coming rain in the air and the wind was moving softly over the fields like quiet footsteps. Rene was right. It's lonely here. Had Oliver spelled out all his actions to her? Given her a blow by blow account of everything that had happened? Or had he kept it brief? "All is taken care of, Rene. A little bloodily. A little messily. But who's to know?"

No one in that isolated place.

Unless . . .

Unless Maeve . . .

There was a fern growing in the crevice of the wall like a green probing hand. I touched it and it was sharp against my fingers. My world seems so small now, a tiny area on a coast road. No one around.

Except Oliver, speaking quietly to his son.

The sound of the van door closing. Will he drive away? Say nothing? Just leave me here? Please, let it be like that.

"Maeve." He touches my shoulder.

I won't turn and look at him.

"He's settled down. Will probably sleep."

He sounds so *normal* still.

"I've told him that he'll be with Rene soon and that cheered him. You needn't be afraid that things won't go well for him – they will. His future depends on Rene keeping out of trouble. I've told her that, time and time again. When we make a new start up North, I believe she will. Another prison sentence and he's smashed back to where he started. He needs her. And he needs me. You understand that, don't you? *He needs me to be there.*"

Yes, I understand that. He has stopped dissembling. I turn now and see what I expected to see. The eyes don't match the calmness in the voice. This is a crisis time for both of us.

How do I answer questions he is afraid to ask?

He tries a devious approach. "Will your mother report that damaged wall in the caravan to the fuzz?"

The obvious answer is no. I'd be crazy if I said yes. But when I do say – no – I mean it. I'll dissuade her from telling anybody.

He relaxes a little. He has sounded me out, listened perhaps for the nuance in my voice. Am I still a mate? Reluctantly, and only to a degree, yes. For Rene's sake and for Wayne's.

He goes on: "You and Wayne have the same sort of imagination. Harmless for him – all that magic button rubbish – not so harmless for you."

A threat?

"You don't know anything, Maeve. If the fuzz come asking questions you can't tell them anything because you don't know anything. Try to be glad that's the way it is."

Imagination is bad enough, memory is a thousand times worse. What will he remember for the rest of his life?

There is a long and very awkward silence.

Broken by the thin yapping of a dog in the distance.

"You could sleep up at the farm tonight," he suggests.

"Why should I?"

"It's better for you to be away from the caravan. If you won't go to the farm, then go home."

It's peremptory.

Go away, Maeve. Out of our lives. Go quickly. And keep your mouth shut.

The unspoken words are harsh inside my head like neon lights.

And then he does the unexpected. He leans over, takes me by the shoulders and kisses me. Lips closed. No passion. But no guile, either. Not a calculated act. A leave-taking with a touch of tenderness.

I watch him as he goes back to Wayne, gets into the van, and drives it down the darkening road. There are tears on my cheeks; I rub at them impatiently. Ashamed.

14

Back in the caravan I sit hunched up in the bottom bunk with the duvet pulled around me for warmth. A mentor, the holier-than-thou part of me that sends me on demos, is whispering about 'moral stance' and 'ethical code'. I can relate them to abhorrence of the bomb and other barbarities, but I can't relate them to Oliver. I should, but I can't.

I thought I knew him, but how can anyone know anyone right down to the gut centre of his being? And if one could, how could one presume to judge?

Murder, for any reason, is unforgivable.

Is it?

Emphatically – yes!

Think of Anna's beautiful face alive – now imagine it dead. Remember the way Rene looked when she was taken into the ambulance. Visualise what happened to Wayne. No – that's unbearable. I can't. *You must.*

Now look at Oliver again.

He had been Horden's prime target. Obviously. But who had been tracking whom? And why had the trail led here? Because of the isolation? A perfect set-up, it must have seemed, with Wayne as the bait. Had there been a violent confrontation, or a quiet killing by stealth? The former is more acceptable to me, but does anything, any circumstance, mitigate the horror of murder? No, how can it? Hug your principles to you, Maeve, as your mentor is telling you.

But perhaps he couldn't help it. Self defence, followed by remorse. Oh, come on! Remember what he said: "It had to be done." He was deeply satisfied. And you know it.

He is so sure of me. And rightly. That wasn't a Judas kiss he gave me, it was an expression of trust. He did it for Anna, for Rene – and above all for Wayne. So I would protect him? Yes. Immoral. Unethical. All right – yes. I have been sliding all the way down the slope since Chornley and it has been an easy ride. Fact? Yes.

Thoughts any clearer now? No.

Conscience eased? Never.

Seek solace in childhood memories, then. Try to be at peace for a while. Coming here to the caravan with family and friends. Wet bathing suits put to dry on the rocks, bright splashes of primary colours on grey stone. Sun always shining, the breezes warm. Mother, not looking much older than I do now, lying on a yellow rug on the grass, reading a book. Or knitting. Father, lithe and athletic, playing cricket on the beach with me. A picture in time, perfect in retrospect, though perhaps not in reality. On the whole, good.

I get up restlessly and walk the length of the caravan, touching surfaces, trying to hold the picture, but it is disintegrating slowly like ancient bones. It won't stay. The ambience now is wrong. How can you dream dreams that are sweet in an execution shed?

He has left his cigarettes and matches on the kitchen table. Deliberately? He mentioned fire insurance earlier. A hint? Why didn't he do it at the time? Probably because there were observers around – Jean and Nick Corby had been walking their dog and had actually knocked at the door. That must have startled him. So he'd tidied the place up as best he could, and mended the bullet hole temporarily so that it wouldn't be noticed.

And gone away to wait.

To wait longer than he expected to because Wayne and I were here.

Everything going wrong.

It's ironical that his child found the evidence that could have put him inside. If a scene of crime team came here to investigate he wouldn't stand a chance. The belt being washed up was bad luck. To miss the cartridge case was careless. He's a bungler. Not of the killer breed. His amateurism consoles me.

But not a lot.

I'm throbbing away inside my head trying to find reasons for doing – or not doing – something that he should have done. Perhaps will do later, if I just go away.

But he may not.

My mother can never come back here again. Must never come. I couldn't bear to think of her here. So do I do it for her and for the memory of my father . . .?

Or . . . for Oliver? To make it safe for him?

My conscience is kicking me for an answer. I quieten it by thinking of Rene. She needs him. So does Wayne. As he so rightly said.

It's called arson. Not a terrible sounding word. Buggery sounds worse than abuse. Execution doesn't sound as bad as murder. It may be the sibilants, they're soft toned. Official statements from unofficial movements use words very cleverly. Reprisals are taken. Informers are despatched. It all sounds clean. Hurting Sutherland wasn't clean. There was blood on his face . . . and mud. And I'm seeing him now, too vividly, and all the guilt is surging through me again.

You can't burn memories, but the tangible can be set alight.

So set the place on fire – but carefully.

Arson is a criminal offence. It has to seem an accident. Families get cremated in their sleep because someone's been careless with a cigarette.

I pick up the packet of cigarettes and hate the look and feel of them. I've never smoked. I can't smoke. Oh yes, you can. You'll shove a lighted cigarette down the side of the sofa and never mind if you cough your lungs out trying to light it. Just do it. *Do it*.

I put one between my lips and pick up the matches. But if it's going to be burnt out eventually why light it in the first place? No one will know. Someone might. Forensic evidence. That fat blonde arsonist in Chornley wouldn't have ended up there if she'd been more careful – remember what she told you about the paraffin rag, left where it shouldn't have been – on the stove?

I light the cigarette. Draw on it. Almost choke.

When I push it down the side of the sofa, it goes out. I light another. It takes three, helped along with pieces of newspaper. Evil little flames start creeping along the cushions and smoke is spiralling, making the air foul.

I pick up my purse and car keys and go outside. My eyes are smarting and my throat is raw. I crouch in the grass trying to breathe.

As the fire gathers strength the caravan looks like a wounded animal under attack. The whole structure seems to be softening, blackening, falling in on itself. There's a crack like a snapping branch and one of the windows blows out. The flames are getting bigger.

The farm dog is barking again, joined by others. Warning yelps that something is amiss. I need to get away before the Corbys are alerted.

My guilt as I leave the field is mixed with a kind of atavistic awe. The fire is becoming splendid. Roaring beyond control. My reasons for starting it no longer seem very important. A great bank of black cloud is merging with the smoke. Celestial disapproval, maybe. Rain that had drizzled earlier now starts falling heavily. I've forgotten to take my mack out of the van and I'm getting soaked. The rain feels marvellous.

It has come just at the right time.

Too late.

It was after midnight when I arrived home. It had been raining here, too, but the moon was clear and the roses looked drowned in silver. It's a beautiful garden. Civilised. Neat. The house was in darkness and the front door barred. Christopher, obviously, had returned and was in bed.

I felt like a rat that had emerged from a sewer – damp – dirty – and no longer euphoric. The elation – the sense of power – had gone. The primitive act of fire raising had set me aglow emotionally, like a glass of strong wine. Now, rather alarmed by the possible consequences, all I wanted was warmth, a stiff drink, and bed.

Sarah might be occupying it.

So what?

After the events of the last few hours I couldn't care if Christopher had a harem of women sleeping all over the place. But it was necessary to get in.

I put my thumb on the bell and kept it there.

He came to the door in his pyjamas, too unrumpled to have been making love. "You're very late, Maeve. I'd stopped expecting you." It sounded censorious but I detected an undertone of relief. I apologised for disturbing him.

"I wasn't asleep. I'm relieved to see you."

He followed me to the dining room and watched me pouring myself a large measure of whisky. The house was warm, but I was shivering and couldn't keep my hand steady. How long is the prison sentence for arson? And if it's arson plus complicity in murder — what then? Life? Did Oliver have a good reason not to set the caravan on fire? When it finally burns down to the ground what might be found under it? Hysteria conjured up mental pictures so bizarre I felt like laughing and weeping at the same time. But did neither.

Christopher asked me quietly what was the matter. Nothing, I told him. Absolutely nothing at all.

I took my drink through to the living room and hoped he would leave me alone for a while. His anxiety added to my guilt. I resented it.

He went upstairs to fetch his dressing-gown and came down wearing the maroon paisley one I'd given him the Christmas before I was put inside. Maybe he took the towelling one to Sarah's and forgot it. He'd put slippers on, too, not the usual scuffed ones, but the soft, dark tan leather ones he'd bought in Paris when he'd bought me the shoes. Paris. A long time ago. Another world. I tried to calm myself by remembering how we were then. He, as always, a pillar of normality, a solid rock. I with no premonition of what was to come.

He sat opposite me and his gaze was intent as if he were trying to get inside my mind. I looked away, guarding my thoughts.

There was a book on the floor by his chair, partially covered by *The Times* folded back at the crossword page. After returning from Sarah's he had probably spent the evening hours reading a definitive biography of someone or other and completing the crossword.

While I . . . While I . . . What has this awful night done to me? What have I done?

He spoke sharply. "Your face is very dirty, Maeve, and you smell of smoke."

I told him that I'd had a bit of bother with the car – a flat tyre. "I had to change it in the rain." The lie came very easily. I hoped he'd forget the smoke.

"You've never changed a tyre in your life."

"Needs must, when there's no one around."

He was worried that I'd been driving in remote areas after dark. "Anything could have happened to you."

"Nothing did. I'm fine."

"Did anything burn in the car – the electrics – the brakes?"

"It was just a puncture. Some stubble had been burnt in the field nearby. That sort of smell clings."

"Are you sure you're all right?"

"Of course." Fine and dandy. Marvellous. Terribly good at pyrotechnics. And a wonderful liar.

I bit my lip and turned my head away, controlling tears.

He must have thought I was still upset about the row we'd had over Wayne and he tried to make amends. "I didn't follow you down to the caravan because you asked me not to."

"It was better for you to stay away."

"If the child's father hadn't shown up when he did, I would have come."

"Yes."

"He seemed a harmless sort of chap."

"Yes."

"Not a lot up top, I would have thought."

He couldn't be referring to Oliver's thick dark hair. "No."

"He's got a job, he told me. Somewhere up north. Labouring, or something."

"In a warehouse."

"He's taking his family with him."

"Yes."

"So that particular episode is over."

Episode – a frail little word – brief – not important. Is that the way he sees it? It's better that he should.

I didn't answer.

He was watching me very keenly. "There's something troubling you." The inquisitorial tone was back. "What is it?"

"Nothing. I'm just feeling tired." I stood up before he could start probing. "It's time for bed."

I had a quick shower and didn't bother protecting my hair; the smell of smoke had to be washed away. I towelled it and then put a dry towel on the pillow in the single bed I'd used when Wayne was with me. I had tidied the duvet on his bed before leaving the house with him but hadn't noticed the Lego tank that had fallen on the floor.

I bent over and picked it up, then sat on my bed holding it. He would be at home by now in bed in that cheerless flat. The cartridge case will have been carefully disposed of. Oliver will have given him a substitute magic button, perhaps, something more button shaped.

Christopher came along the corridor and stood at the door. "Do you intend spending the night in here?"

"My hair is wet. It's better that I should."

He didn't try to persuade me to join him but offered to fetch my hair dryer. "It's unwise to go to bed with damp hair."

Many things I do are unwise, going to bed with damp hair is the least of them. I told him I couldn't be bothered. "I'm too tired."

He looked at me mutely, then moved restlessly around the room, pausing by the bedside table. He took the phone off the hook. "Some of the neighbours have been having night-time calls. Your being in prison seems to have stirred up a hornets' nest in the district. The criminal fraternity are targeting on it. It was peaceful enough before." He smiled wryly. "Sorry. Joke. Not a good one. Did you have any worrying calls while I was away?"

It was easier to say no than yes. I hadn't even the energy to think about it. Chummy or somebody else, put in context, didn't matter very much. If anyone rang tonight it would be the fire service or the police, if they'd been alerted by the Corbys. I'd handle that in the morning as best I could.

Christopher said that the colonel was going ex-directory and he thought we'd better do the same for a while.

I shrugged. "If that's what you want."

He came and sat beside me on the bed. "Everything would be much easier for both of us if I could understand what you want. It has always been your nature to be impulsive. Your unfortunate friendship with the Dudgeons was just that. You rushed into it without thought. Now that they're going you should be able to settle down again and start behaving with more maturity."

Maturity? Yes, a fair comment, perhaps. We've never bridged the ten-year age gap between us. But I resent 'unfortunate'. How can a friendship be fortunate or unfortunate? It's made up of good and bad and grows the only way it can. Impulsive? Yes. Emotion dictates what I do most of the time. Is there anyone so controlled that emotion plays no part? Cold blooded killers, perhaps. Horden, in prison, planning his revenge on Anna. I see very clearly the mug shots of him and Anna on Inspector Grange's desk. An ordinary-looking man. A good-looking woman. I won't try to visualise how they looked . . . afterwards. I'm troubled enough by what I've seen. Rene's face, cut and bleeding, as she was carried out on the stretcher. Wayne, crouching over the belt, terrified. Oliver, the avenger. Avenger. An acceptable word. A cloak and dagger image. If it helps then cling to it. It does help – a little.

Christopher is looking at the Lego toy in my hand. He reaches for it, takes it from me, and puts it on the table next to the silent telephone. "The child has gone, Maeve. Stop thinking of him."

His action annoys me. He shouldn't have done that. Can't he understand that I need to hold it, to think with tenderness of the good parts of the friendship, that losing Wayne will be tearing part of me away?

I take it and hold it again.

He flushes with sudden anger. "For Christ's sake! Your obsession with the child, the family, the whole sordid affair, is sick." He gets up and walks over to the window and stands looking out into the darkness. Eventually, in command of himself again,

161

he turns back to me. "You've been out of prison seven months – surely long enough for the trauma to heal, if it ever heals. Perhaps it doesn't. We can't go on like this. We have to talk – about ourselves – the future. But not tonight. Tomorrow, when you're less tired."

Oh yes, I think. Tomorrow. We'll talk tomorrow. You'll learn about the caravan and you'll stop believing my lies. You're right – prison isn't something you recover from. Nothing is ever the same again. It's like being trapped on a roller-coaster of events you can't control. Or perhaps *you* could, Christopher, with your sane way of looking at everything, not that you'd do anything that would put you inside in the first place. I'm bad for you, and you're not good for me, though you try to be.

He checks the bedside clock with his watch. "It's running slow. It's twenty past one." He adjusts it, then smiles stiffly at me in an attempt to be conciliatory. "Don't get up too early. Sleep as long as you want to."

At the door he pauses, seems embarrassed. "I haven't been spending the last few days with Sarah – as you seem determined to believe. And we'll talk about that in the morning, too."

He avoids my eyes and leaves me, closing the door behind him before I can think of an answer.

I sit for a long time on the edge of the bed, clutching Wayne's toy. The room, with the door closed, seems cell-like and claustrophobic. But this door can be opened again.

And so can Christopher's, down the corridor.

Or can it?

Maybe not any more. And I lack the will to try.

Epilogue

Today is my twenty-eighth birthday and the anniversary of my release from Chornley.

Twelve months of freedom.

It's a frosty morning. One of those pretty days when the sky is a deep strong blue. I stand by the bedroom window and admire the February garden, crisp bushes, brave early flowers, a milky sheen over everything. It seems more than a year since that other frosty morning when Christopher brought me home and I wandered outside for a while, trying to get the feel of the place, trying to belong again.

Living alone these last few months has taken a little while to get used to, but it has its compensations. I shall spend my birthday doing exactly what I want to do without excuse or apology.

I take a long hot bath and dress in thermal underwear and a thick green tracksuit. It's going to be cold standing around.

The postman came early and there are lots of cards waiting for me on the mat. I take them to the kitchen and open them after I've had coffee. A flowery one from my mother: "Have a lovely day, darling." Oh, I will. I'll be meeting her for lunch tomorrow. We've become closer recently despite her disapproval of the break-up of my marriage. I have let a good man go, she tells me, why in the name of reason let another woman get her hands on him? Because the hands are Hester's, I tell her, and Hester is right for him.

They were introduced at a masonic charity concert, he told me. One I had refused to attend during my antisocial period. She's a freelance graphic artist and had designed the posters and programmes. I remembered meeting her some while afterwards at Eric's. A tall, fair haired woman with brown eyes and a very gentle way of speaking – rather hesitant – rather shy. She gave the impression of having no strong feelings about anything. Apart from Christopher. Even then, had I looked for it, I would have seen it. She'll love him, as he deserves to be loved, feed him well, not throw bricks at demos, or embarrass him in any way. He extolled her virtues on that autumn morning following my night of arson, five months ago, and confessed he'd slept with her for the first time when he'd left home on account of my taking in 'that child'. I think he was hurt rather than relieved that I didn't rail at him, or appear in any way appalled. But how could I? I was nervously expecting the police to come calling with a warrant for my arrest. They didn't, but I wasn't to know. Arson is a crime, adultery isn't. In Christopher's case, given the provocation, it isn't even a sin.

His birthday present for me, a silver brooch with a lapis lazuli centre, arrived yesterday, a day early, posted from Switzerland where he and Hester are holidaying together. He shouldn't be giving me expensive gifts now we're apart. Sarah would never have let him. They will probably be less expensive as time goes on and his conscience heals. Despite all my reassurances that going our separate ways is the best thing for both of us he still looks troubled whenever we meet. And I'm not as indifferent as I pretend. He has always been good to me. Once the house is sold and the proceeds shared the break will become easier. I'll put down fresh roots somewhere else. As he has.

The other cards are from friends I've known a long time, and from colleagues at the small, new publishing company where I do the accounts, answer the phone, and act as general dogsbody. We totter on the edge of bankruptcy most of the time, awaiting the blockbuster novel that never arrives, but manage optimistically to survive.

I notice one card amongst the others, a postcard with a picture of Blackpool tower on it, but postmarked Newcastle four days ago. The sprawling writing is familiar: *"Can't remember dates, but think it was about this time last year. Goodbye screws! I haven't said hello to them since. Lucky me!! Sorry I haven't been in touch. All three of us are well. Wayne still talks about you. Can read your Dad's books by himself now. We all send heaps of love. Rene."*

A small hard lump positioned somewhere at the base of my throat suddenly makes swallowing difficult, and then it begins to throb and soften and melt as I weep with relief. The long period of silence has been broken. The anxiety I've lived with ever since that evening when Oliver drove off with Wayne has been dispelled. He is safe with his father.

And Oliver, it seems, is safe from the police. Horden's body has never been found. Perhaps never will be. There are times when I talk myself into believing that he's out there – somewhere – alive. That all those explanations Oliver gave me in the caravan are true. According to the Corbys there had been deer poaching going on at a reserve a few miles inland. Poachers could have broken into the caravan and used it as a temporary base. One of their rifles might have been fired accidentally – hence the bullet hole. And the smell could have been rotting venison. It's plausible. Why not believe it? Most of the time I do. My explanation about the cigarette causing the fire in the caravan was believed by those who mattered; the ones who could have slammed a charge of arson on me. The others, Christopher and my mother, voiced their scepticism only to me. An aberrant action, I told them. I wouldn't smoke again.

I gather up the birthday cards and arrange them around the living room. Rene's postcard I touch gently as if I'm touching her hand. I can imagine what she'd say to me if she were here now, and how she'd say it with a mixture of amusement and disbelief. "Shit, Maeve, you're going out to do *what*?"

Macbarra said he'd meet me with the others at Trafalgar Square. He's been away most of the week recording a programme about

165

the Benedictine monastery at Lindisfarne. Today's demo isn't Mac's scene at all, but the television people are going along and he's taking his mike for the radio broadcast. There'll be a lot of media people there, stars of stage and screen, plus a few loonies like me. His words, but spoken with affection.

We have lunched together a few times, and this evening we're having a birthday dinner at a Greek restaurant. Nowhere expensive. In this modern age of multiple commitment he has two young sons by his first marriage to support. As yet we haven't slept together. The relationship grows slowly and gives us both a measure of contentment.

I have to take the car despite parking problems. The banner would be a nuisance in a bus or the tube. The meeting is scheduled for midday and by giving myself plenty of time I manage to arrive at eleven forty-five. Crowds have already gathered and the police are there to keep order. I remember that other protest meeting at Langdon village where Sergeant Sutherland and his colleagues were doing the best they could. Feelings then ran higher. Today we're concerned, but not for ourselves, the issue is not so large, not cataclysmic. I doubt anyone will be hurt. Not here. A young bobby catches my eye and smiles at me. I smile back. I've started to re-discover their humanity. They're not a breed apart.

An elderly man comments to no one in particular that it's a good day for this sort of thing. No wind. A slim young woman with cropped sandy hair says she hasn't a banner and may she help hold mine? We unfurl it together, but when she sees it she says it's no damned good. Too pretty. No blood.

I don't tell her I have an aversion to blood. That CND emblem drawn in blood and pushed through my letter-box is unforgettable. She leaves me holding my mild, pretty banner on my own and finds another more suitable.

Mac eventually joins me. His nose is pink with the cold and his breath spirals in frosty clouds. He says a hot coffee wouldn't come amiss. I tell him – later. We have to do our chanting first. I find this part of the demo rather embarrassing and he regards me with amusement while I get on with it. Some of the spectators join in, a few boo, ribald remarks are hurled, but most seem sympathetic.

One of Mac's team comes over and asks if I'd like to say a few words. I tell him to get someone more important, that I'm not news these days, thank God. Mac agrees and tells his colleague not to press it. My anonymity is cosy. I'm clothed, not stripped naked any more.

The police give the demo half an hour, which is probably quite generous, before moving us along. I hope it will be effective. We're trying to protect the helpless. The cause is a good one.

Mac and I go to a nearby restaurant, a pleasant, cosy little place with stripped pine furniture and yellow tablecloths. He fetches coffee at the counter while I park my banner behind the coat stand. He has a small parcel, I notice, when I rejoin him at the table. It's for me, he tells me, a birthday present suitable for the occasion.

He watches while I unwrap the toy – a small white baby seal like the one on my banner. "They don't all die in polluted seas," he says, "or get clubbed to death on land. Disasters like the 1988 virus don't occur all that often and there are always survivors, no matter what. If they weren't such appealing creatures I doubt if you'd have been out there today waving that banner of yours."

I fondle the seal, delighted with it, and tell him he's an appalling cynic.

He grins and doesn't deny it. "You're no great hand as an artist. But the kids in the crowds liked your seal. I suppose the demo will raise some cash. What will it be used for? Research into viral disease of aquatic mammals? Or is it a campaign against the toxic oceans?"

"Both probably. I don't know."

"Well, you should. You're an impractical crusader, Maeve, trying to set an imperfect world to rights. Maybe that's why I like you." He changes the subject. "How's the lad? The one whose mother was your friend at Chornley."

I run my fingers through the soft white wool. "Loved and happy," I tell him with complete conviction. "The Dudgeons are excellent parents. They moved to Newcastle a few months ago. Oliver has a job. Wayne goes to school. Rene says he can read now. Everything is okay for him at last."

I expect him to be pleased, but he's frowning. "What did you say the name was?"

"Wayne. Do you remember the paper animals you were making for him and he . . .?"

"The surname. You hadn't mentioned it before."

Hadn't I? No, probably not. I usually spoke of them as Rene – Oliver – Wayne. He's looking at me as if I've committed a gross breach of etiquette by not telling him. "Dudgeon," I say. "Like the character in Shaw's play."

"Oh, Christ!" He pushes his coffee cup aside as if it's laced with arsenic.

"What's the matter?"

His eyes have narrowed with distress. "What a hell of a thing to have to tell you."

"What do you mean? What are you getting at?"

The atmosphere of the café is changing. It's too full of people – all eating – talking – rattling cutlery. There's a groundswell of noise getting louder and the air is thick with the smell of over-spiced food, bitter curry, greasy chips, slimy vegetables.

He pulls his chair a little closer to the table, looks uneasily at me, and then away. The waitress, a plump girl in a green dress, covered with a frilly yellow apron, thinks he's trying to catch her eye and comes over. "Can I get you anything, sir?"

He shakes his head. Looks back at me.

"You know I was in Lindisfarne earlier this week doing a radio programme?"

"And so?"

"On my way back I spent Thursday night at Newcastle. There was a full spread about it in the local paper."

"About what, for God's sake?" My hands are beginning to tremble.

He leans across and takes them in his. The signet ring on his little finger presses hard into my skin. "Apparently your friend, Mrs. Dudgeon – Rene – had returned home after a day's shopping on Wednesday afternoon. Her husband had finished work early and helped her carry her packages inside. There was what the paper called a 'domestic fracas' which became violent. One of the neighbours called the police. Unfortunately they arrived too late."

Too late?

His ring is hurting me. I want it to hurt more. To press

168

harder. Harder. Concentrate on the pressure. Harder. Harder. Pain.

He loosens the grip, but keeps holding my hands. "The paper was careful in its wording, but it was easy to read between the lines. A woman who lived in an adjoining house said they seemed a happy, united family, devoted to the little boy. That seemed the general opinion, but another neighbour insinuated that Mrs. Dudgeon had been battered on previous occasions."

There's a thin, high buzzing in my head and for a while I hear nothing else. He keeps on talking – talking – but the words are just meaningless sounds. A shaft of sunlight falls across the table, but the world is black. And cold.

Oliver's voice, low but very clear, whispers words from the past: *Wayne needs me . . . He needs us both . . . Another prison sentence and he's smashed back to where he started . . . I've told her that, time and time again . . .*

Smashed . . . Wayne . . . tender, loving . . . Wayne, yes . . . but Rene . . .

Mac is mouthing something about being sorry. "Shouldn't have told you about it here – should have waited until we were alone together somewhere – at my flat – or your place."

I tell him it's not true, that I heard from her today, that I don't believe it. Or I think I tell him. Maybe I haven't spoken. I'm not sure. Either way, I do believe it. The card was posted four days ago – on Tuesday.

I look around me. Why is everyone behaving so calmly? What kind of bland, untroubled lives do these other people lead? How can they sit and eat and grin and swill their drinks and talk – and talk – while Rene . . . This is the most inimical, abominable place I've ever been in.

Mac's fingers, warm on my cold hands, are stroking them very gently. What is he trying to prove? That we're alive – can touch – feel – be?

When Rene wrote the card she was so happy – everyone well – goodbye screws, not said hello since – typical Rene – and then – afterwards – one day later – she – Oliver – sometime on Wednesday afternoon –

I pull my hands away and my wrist catches the edge of my

169

coffee cup. The brown liquid splashes over the white coat of the toy seal. A dark stain appears like old blood. Why do they say cull when they mean kill? What had Oliver said to the police – that he'd culled her? That he'd culled Rene. What had she stolen – a white seal fur? I pick up the toy and hold it close to me. It's sodden and coffee drips through my fingers. I'll wash it. Wayne will like it when it's clean. Mac points out that it's staining my tracksuit, and the tablecloth, and leans across the table to take it from me. I back away. Christopher had tried to take the Lego toy away, too, all those months ago. Why does everyone try to separate me from the child? This toy is for him. When I go to him. Soon.

Mac dabs at the stained cloth, using one of the yellow paper napkins. He speaks slowly as if he's choosing his words with care. I sense he's trying to console me. "If what the neighbour hinted about his battering her before is true, there might be mitigating circumstances. The charge could be manslaughter – not murder."

None of this makes any sense. Mitigating because he made a habit of it? How many times would he have to beat her up to be acquitted?

He puts the wet napkin on his plate. "This kind of tragedy has happened so many times before. It's natural for a woman to retaliate by grabbing any defensive weapon that comes to hand. It was unfortunate that she grabbed a knife. An ordinary kitchen knife might not have done much harm, but this one penetrated. He died in hospital a couple of hours after she stabbed him. She was charged on Thursday and there was a paragraph in the tabloids yesterday. The northern papers will have carried more details."

I look at him with total incomprehension, then get up abruptly, clumsily, and my chair overturns. The waitress comes across, picks it up, and starts complaining about the stains on the cloth. This is ordinary, I can deal with her anger. But not with the other. The other, what I've just been told, won't get inside my head. I tell her rudely and loudly what to do with the cloth. People are staring at me. I stare back. They're like creatures under water, out of focus.

Mac is saying something conciliatory to the waitress. Apologising for me. Says I'm not well. Maybe. Maybe not. My throat and chest are aflame and my breathing is becoming slow and laboured, and hurts. I walk unsteadily into the entrance hall and collect the banner. Someone's scarf has fallen across it, a woollen one. I put the scarf back on the peg. It's red and black, the same colours Rene and I used on the jumper we both half made. At Chornley.

I go outside.

The sun looks like an embolus. A red clot in the afternoon sky. The day seems all wrong. Askew. Not right.

I stand by the shop next to the restaurant. The window is full of electrical goods. Things to wash with, clean with, listen to. Gadgets whirring away. In people's houses. All the time. Busy world. Busy, domesticated world. There's a microwave oven at the front of the window. Like the one Rene wanted to sell me the first day I visited her flat. Off the back of a lorry? *Oh, Maeve, Maeve, how the sweet hell did I put up with you all those bloody months! If I wanted to flog stolen property I wouldn't flog it to you. We're mates, aren't we? Mates . . . mates . . .*

And Oliver: *We don't take charity from our friends.*

And Wayne: *I'll rub my magic button . . . make you come.*

A mean little wind has started to blow and my banner has become loose from one of the supporting sticks. It's flapping near my face like the butterfly had flapped near Wayne's.

Oliver's tenderness that day on the beach when he had held him in his arms. His controlled anger as he had slashed away at Horden's belt and warned Wayne not to come too close in case the knife slipped.

Was that the knife Rene had used?

It must have been.

Why did he keep something so ugly – so dangerous? What possible need could he have had for it? A murder weapon, as lethal as a gun, too easily come by in time of stress.

What will Rene tell the judge when she's on trial? Will she make things easier for herself by saying that he made a habit of attacking her violently and that she was terrified of him? Or will she say something flippant – as she had to me – about wanting to stay in one piece? A simple confession: "I didn't mean to do it. I loved him, but he was hurting me," might sound implausible to

171

the jury, but could be the nearest to the truth. For most of the time they were happy together.

One day she might tell me. All of it.

Will she do time in Holloway, or in a northern prison? The women's wing at Durham, perhaps?

She feels so close to me now I could be wearing her skin, going through everything with her again. The routine of committal – a listing of possessions – you may keep this – you can't have that. The medical. Long, bleak corridors. The sound of doors being locked on the landings at night. I can hear them. See the peep-holes. Never any privacy. The unlocking in the morning – grey mornings of grey days that go on and on. A withering of confidence. Do this. Do that. Don't think. Emasculation of the will. Self respect has to be coaxed to grow again like a tender plant. Or it had to for me. Was it like that for Rene?

Not when she was in Chornley with me – no. That was an easier régime, the worst was over. Her crime was a game – a game she lost now and then. But now it will be different. I maimed a man I didn't know and I'm so sorry – so sorry – so sorry. It will be worse for Rene.

A year ago today Oliver was picking her up outside Chornley and she was clutching him around the waist as they went zooming off on his motorbike. I envied them their reunion, they were so pleased to be together. Christopher and I were so stiff and awkward. With Oliver and Rene there was just obvious delight.

If only we could all start again. Alter the scenario. Blot out twelve months of change, frightening and irreversible. For Rene the pain will be ongoing, the remorse hard to bear.

"How will she cope? How can she stand it? What will she do?"

I wasn't aware that I'd spoken aloud, or that Mac was standing beside me looking very concerned.

"People are resilient, Maeve, even in the most appalling of situations. It's the children who can't cope. They're the vulnerable ones."

Of course – Wayne. Oliver's sentiments. Precisely what he would say. Has said.

I tell Mac that I'll take the train to Newcastle tomorrow and bring him back home with me.

He seems startled and doesn't answer for a moment. The pause is full of doubt. "You can't just walk in and do that. He'll have been taken into care. After that it's up to his mother to say what's to happen to him."

I think of Anna. The truth about Wayne's background will be known soon, but I won't divulge it.

"Rene would want him to come to me. She and Oliver have spent the last few years avoiding the Social Services."

He can't understand that. "They're conscientious people doing a difficult job the best way they can. They'll be good to him."

"But he needs to be with someone he knows – someone who loves him. I love him. He loves me. He said so."

"Maybe, but it's not that simple." The comment is dry, dismissive. He sounds like Christopher.

There are people passing us, up and down the pavement, a thrusting mass. There is too much noise. Too much confusion. My clear-cut reasons for doing what seems to me the only right thing to do are being questioned by this man I thought would be compassionate to a child. Instead he tells me that I'm not in a fit state to think rationally. "You can't make plans, Maeve. For the boy. For yourself. Not yet. Come back to my flat and rest awhile. You're not safe to drive your car. You can drive to your home later when you're calmer. Or I'll drive you. Come home with me now."

His flat. My home. I don't want to go anywhere. Both places seem alien. There is no one I can turn to. I start walking away, pushing past people with my banner, muttering apologies if I bump into them. The air is rank with the smell of petrol and loud with the roar of traffic.

He catches up with me and takes the banner from me. "You'll brain somebody. Where are you going? My flat's in the other direction."

I don't know where I'm going. Anywhere. I don't answer. Keep walking.

He puts his hand on my arm and stops me. "Maeve! I feel like a crass idiot holding this. Presumably you don't. That's where we differ. Take it back." He furls it and gives it to me.

When he speaks again his voice is less brusque. "This isn't the best of places to talk, but that can't be helped, so stand still and listen. If you intend starting a crusade for the child, to try to get possession, I doubt you'll succeed, but it will be the best cause you've lost. You've been in prison, and that's a hell of an obstacle for a start. It shouldn't be – in your case – but it is. You'd care for that little lad a damned sight better than anyone else. I know that. But would the authorities? I don't want to see you hurt. Any more than you want to see the child hurt. What I'm trying to say is . . . if you're determined to press on with this, after you've given yourself more time to think, then go ahead. You'll give him friendship and love. No one can stop that. But don't burn your heart out if you can't do any more. And if things get rough, and you want support, someone to do battle on your behalf and Wayne's, then shout for me. I like the little lad, too."

We're standing on the pavement in the Strand and I'm crying. Mac puts his arm around my shoulders and for a moment or two holds me close to him. "The child," he says gently, "will survive."

I believe it. Friendship and love will do for a start. We'll take it from there.

FOR THE BEST IN PAPERBACKS, LOOK FOR THE 🐧

Jctn West Best Western   9   10   18

Oregon Aub   43   47

2-05 - 354 -2363

Sat 24th note arrive

thru 30th last

note